MORE THAN MAGIC

Kathryn Lasky

Illustrated by Ricardo Tercio

WENDY
LAMB
BOOKS

Text copyright © 2016 by Kathryn Lasky
Jacket and interior illustrations copyright © 2016 by Ricardo Tercio

All rights reserved. Published in the United States by Wendy Lamb Books, an imprint of Random House Children's Books, a division of Penguin Random House LLC, New York.

Wendy Lamb Books and the colophon are trademarks of Penguin Random House LLC.

Visit us on the Web! randomhousekids.com

Educators and librarians, for a variety of teaching tools, visit us at RHTeachersLibrarians.com

Library of Congress Cataloging-in-Publication Data
Name: Lasky, Kathryn, author.
Title: More than magic / Kathryn Lasky.
Description: First edition. | New York : Wendy Lamb Books, [2016] | Summary: "Ryder always thought something special would happen when she turned eleven, and this year she misses her mom, who died several years ago, more than ever. Ryder's parents created a cartoon show featuring an eleven-year-old hero named Rory. Then on Ryder's eleventh birthday, Rory steps out of the screen—Rory needs help!"— Provided by publisher.
Identifiers: LCCN 2015031864 | ISBN 9780553498912 (trade : alk. paper) | ISBN 978-0-553-49892-9 (lib. bdg. : alk. paper) | ISBN 978-0-553-49893-6 (ebook) | ISBN 978-0-553-49894-3 (pbk. : alk. paper)
Subjects: | CYAC: Grief—Fiction. | Cartoon characters—Fiction. | Cartoons and comics—Fiction. | Magic—Fiction.
Classification: LCC PZ7.L3274 Mq 2016 | DDC [Fic]—dc23

The text of this book is set in 13-point Apollo.
Interior design by Trish Parcell

Printed in the United States of America
10 9 8 7 6 5 4 3 2 1
First Edition

For those two animation geniuses—Simon Whiteley and Grant Freckelton—who brought "Owls in Helmets" to life and truly inspired this story

PART I

RYDER

The Most Miserable Birthday—*Everrr* . . .

"Happy birthday, dear Ryder!" The eleven birthday candles and the one to grow on barely flicker on my cake. I look around our table. Everyone is smiling and cheering, but underneath, no one is happy. Not my dad. Not our family friend Cassie Simon, and not my pal Eli Weckstein. Two important people are missing from my party. The first is my best friend, Penny, who just moved from California to London. I look down at my cell phone. I thought she would call and wish me happy birthday, or text me. But she hasn't. I guess it's already tomorrow in London. Maybe she got confused. The second person missing from the party is my mom.

My mom, Andrea Holmsby, one of the greatest

animators ever—and I mean *everrr*—died unexpectedly about two years ago. She gave birth to me, Ryder Eloise Holmsby. Her beautiful brain gave birth to Rory, a TV character. Mom and Dad worked together at Starlight Movie Studios, where they made *Super-Rory-Us,* Rory's cartoon show. Rory is based on me, but that's a secret, because Mom and Dad wanted to protect me. Viewers wouldn't guess the connection because Rory and I don't really look alike. Rory the cartoon has brown hair like mine, but hers is curly. My hair is straight, and I'm cursed with a thousand cowlicks. I always look as if I have a Category 5 hurricane blowing around my head. Rory's snub nose is upturned. Mine is sharp. I have gray eyes and Rory's are brown. We each have a freckle on our thumb, and Rory does have certain expressions that are exactly like mine—like what Dad calls my NE: nonnegotiable expression.

My parents thought up Rory in Deadwood, South Dakota, when they were living with Mom's mother, Granny Ryder, after they graduated from art school. Mom was expecting me, but they weren't expecting Rory. She just showed up. An inspiration. The most important thing about Rory is that she's a hero. Rory fights crime. She fights injustice. She sticks up for the little guys and sticks it to the baddies. In short, she kicks butt!

Rory lives in Ecalpon, which is No Place spelled backward. Ecalpon is a bit like Scotland. The time period is a little bit Robin Hood–ish.

I have been eleven for fourteen hours. I was born at six o'clock in the morning West Coast time. Rory started her animated life as an eleven-year-old when I was five. Today is our only overlapping birthday. I always thought amazing things would happen on this day.

As I blow out the candles on the cake, I'm sort of out of wishes. Dad and I look at each other and I know he's thinking about Mom. I think he might be out of wishes too. But then his eyes sparkle and we smile at each other.

When we get home, I turn on the TV in my bedroom. Rory fills the screen: a rerun, one of the last episodes Mom worked on. Rory's climbing the wall of a stone tower to the Witch of Wenham's secret chambers. She swings across the tower's outer wall to a high, narrow window. It's dizzying to watch as she dangles a hundred feet in the air, but she easily makes it to the window and slithers into a secret chamber where the witch does horrible experiments. A rock sits in a birdcage, not a bird. But that rock was once a lovely barn owl. The witch plans on turning it into gold. She's crazy for gold—she's tried turning a mouse into gold, then a rabbit, and now an owl.

I sigh as I watch Rory, and think: *I've caught up with you. At last I'm eleven, just like you.*

Rory approaches the birdcage. Am I imagining it, or is Rory distracted for a split second? Do her eyes flash directly to me? She's undoing the witch's magic by reciting the original spell—*Oh, owl so white and bright, make gold for me tonight*—backward. So Rory says *thginot em rof dlog ekam thgirb dna etihw os lwo ho*. That takes a lot of concentration! But I swear she looks at me just when she reverses the word *make* into *ekam*. That glance can't have been in the script. It's not like Rory gets to decide; she doesn't have free will. People draw her, write for her. She's a cartoon!

"Shazam!" we both cry. That's Rory's special magic word for when she makes things happen.

The rock melts into a beautiful and surprised barn owl. Then the bird spreads its tawny wings and flies out the window of the stone tower. Free!

Rory gives a little salute to the owl as it flies off.

Salute me. Look at me, Rory! I want to say. *It's our birthday. We're both eleven.*

Dad comes in to kiss me good night. "Oh, that one," he says as I turn off the TV. He sinks down on my bed. "Your mom always loved barn owls. The only owls with black eyes, I think. Mom had more plans for that owl." He sighs. "You know, Ryder . . . I . . . I think that maybe I haven't been the—"

"Don't say you haven't been a good dad."

"I've been a mopey dad."

"I've been a mopey daughter."

"Yeah, well . . ." He pauses. "But with the Rory film, I've been—so distracted."

"If you're talking about how you forgot to pick me up last week after pottery class, don't worry about it."

"I do worry about it. It's like I misplaced my brain!" Dad pretends to pop open his brain and put it on my nightstand. I giggle.

"It was the first week of summer vacation. Don't be so hard on yourself. We're both losing our brains a little." I pretend to put my brain next to his. We both laugh.

"I'm going to do better, I promise. The class at the Inner Radiance Meditation Center is helping me a bit. It helps people with a lot of things, like grief."

"Well, that's good, Dad."

"Yes. I've signed up for a few more sessions. . . . And how are you doing? It's hard not having Mom here, isn't it?"

I nod.

"I was thinking, how would you like to spend a few weeks with Granny Ryder out in Deadwood?"

"Really, Dad?" I squeeze my eyes shut and see Granny and me horseback riding. The flash of the sun on the river. The little stone house where Mom grew up . . . and best of all, Granny!

"Yes, really. I called her tonight after we got home from your party. I'll miss you so much, Ryder. But you and Granny will have fun riding, and doing all the things you love to do there. Granny can't wait to see you. I'll finish up the movie, and when you come back, you and I can spend much more time together."

He strokes my hair and I nod. "That sounds good."

"Maybe . . . maybe . . ."

"Yeah, Dad?"

"Well, I know this is an important birthday for you. You're Rory's age now." My eyes widen. I didn't realize that Dad felt the way I do. "You were born in Deadwood Community Hospital. And Mom thought up Rory in Deadwood. So it seems kind of fitting that you go back."

"To our birthplace!"

I jump up and hug him as hard as I can. He hugs back. I tell him, "Dad, I'll miss you. Every minute. I promise I'll be back in time for the movie opening."

"Of course you will!" He kisses the top of my head. "You have to be there."

"So when do I go?"

"Tomorrow?"

"Yes!"

CHAPTER 1

Deadwood

The sun slides like a dull copper coin behind a sky filled with dust as Granny and I ride our horses through the valley. All you can hear is the squeak of our saddles and the horses' hooves on the hard-packed dirt.

"Dust storm coming up the valley," Granny says. A minute later two whirlwinds peel off from the storm. Granny tugs her scarf up to cover her mouth and keep the dust out. Skinny as a split rail, my grandmother sits tall in the saddle. I tug up my scarf too. "Let's pull a Calamity," she says.

Calamity, the sorrel mare that Granny rides, is named for Calamity Jane, the most famous person who ever lived in Deadwood, South Dakota. She was a master of terrific escapes from everything from bad guys to weather. I am behind Granny on my pinto pony, Delbert. The human Delbert was a leading citizen of Deadwood. He and his wife, Delberta, invented the Delbert ice cream bar, chocolate and vanilla all in one. Delbert and Delberta became very rich and my mom went to art school on a D&D scholarship.

Granny digs the heels of her boots into her mare's flanks and gallops down into a steep gorge to escape the marauding dust devils that have multiplied into four swirling cones. By the time we're safe in the gorge, it starts to rain.

"Over here, Ryder!"

Granny finds a ledge with an overhang to protect us. The rain is bucketing down, and when I reach her, my flat-brimmed cowboy hat is spilling sheets of water down my neck and face.

"Why, you're wet as an old wet hen." She chuckles. Granny has a funny little gap between her front teeth that makes her smile extra sweet. She whistles through that gap.

I'm so happy to be riding with Granny on the prairie. Dad was right; this visit was a good idea. Every time he calls, he sounds brighter. Last night he said he had been out to dinner a few times with a lady named Bernice, who is the director of the Radiance place. He said it to me gently, as if I might be worried that he was dating someone. But it's okay. For the first time in almost two years, Dad and I are both sort of happy.

"You know, it was right here that a rattler dropped down on your mom when she was a kid," Granny says.

"What!"

"Yes siree Bob, right over there." She nods toward a rusty patch of stone.

"What did she do?"

"Took her piggin' string and whupped the daylights out of it."

"Piggin' string? But that's what calf ropers use to tie up calves' feet."

"Works on a rattler too. She gave it a few mean swats, then, Lord knows how, but she looped that string round his head and slip-knotted it. Nearly took his whole head off. His rattles are hanging up in the living room—the very ones."

"The ones with the little decorations painted on them?"

"Yes indeed. There wasn't anything your mom couldn't paint or draw on. What an artist! And everything she touched with her paintbrush or her pen—every piece of her art, including all those lovely hats she made with the chicken feathers—they all had soul. Just pure soul." She sighs. "And you, Ryder, were as much of an inspiration as any old bad-butt rattlesnake."

"Granny, I'm not sure that's a compliment."

"Believe me, it is, dollin'."

Nobody says "darling" the way Granny does. Granny's other term of endearment for me is "chicken." Not that she thinks I'm chicken like being afraid of stuff. No, she has a sweet spot for chickens. She raises the prettiest ones—Rhode Island Reds, New Zealand spotted guinea hens. That's where my mom got all the feathers for her hat designs. I have two of the spotted guinea feathers in my hatband. Granny has a Golden Polish in hers.

The rain lets up after about ten minutes and we ride out into the newly rinsed world. It's always beautiful after a downpour. A soft mist rises from the river and curls like a ribbon through the valley. Birds sing, and golden light washes out of the sky. The air is clean and the grass has a tangy sweetness. I bet the earthworms are doing little jigs under the ground.

It isn't long before we see the house crouching under the only grove of cottonwoods on a huge plain. I love Granny's house. A bunch of Mom's things are here. Granny lets me take anything I want. But I don't like taking things back to our house in California. I'm afraid they'd get homesick. Like the patchwork quilt Mom made that I always sleep under here.

Mom was a wonderful quilter. I love the small patches

of cloth that she picked out and carefully stitched together into what's called a crazy quilt, with odd shapes
colliding, unexpected fabrics next to each other, like
velvet next to plain gingham, and all sorts of stitches,
from curlicue embroidery to delicate feather stitches.
There might be fun things besides fabric—beads, lace,
ribbons, buttons, medals, and maybe a feather or two.
She did many patterns, but crazy quilts were her favorite. And they're mine too.

In our house in Bel Air, outside of Los Angeles,
things are too bright, too perfect. There's a swimming
pool where the water looks like blue Jell-O, and the air-
conditioning thrums all day and all night. The grass is
too green and has no smell. The ice maker in the refrig-
erator sounds like bones crunching. But it was Mom and
Dad's dream house. Once I asked Mom how the Bel Air
house could be her dream house when she also said that
about Granny's little stone house. She said, "Nothing
wrong with having a lot of dreams, sweetie."

But you can only live in one dream, I think. Granny's
house is mine. It's all on one level with a wraparound
porch. The porch has what they call out here a brush
arbor roof so the sun doesn't broil you during the day
and the moonlight can trickle through at night. No lawn.
Granny says it's immoral to feed a lawn when children
are starving all over the world. But the best thing is she
has a garden growing right out of her roof. She has a sod

roof, just like Laura Ingalls Wilder did in *Little House on the Prairie*. All kinds of stuff sprouts from that roof, and it's my job to tend it. We don't plant anything, the flowers just come—oxeye daisies; dame's rocket with its soft purple bursts of blossoms; Queen Anne's lace; beardtongue, which doesn't have a beard or tongue but looks like teensy-weensy trumpets for mice to toot. We don't mind the weeds. We like to go up there for star watching.

When we get home from our ride, we unsaddle the horses and brush them down. Granny gives them each a groat cake. Calamity especially loves groat cakes. It's time for our supper, but first I want to see Mom's painted rattles again.

In the living room, I look at the picture of Granny presenting my mom with her diploma. Mom looks slightly embarrassed. It must have been weird to have your own mother be the principal of your school. And there they are—eight rattles. "Holy moly, they're huge!"

"Yep," says Granny. "Look how pretty she painted them. They might be huge rattles for a rattlesnake, but they're kind of a small canvas for a painter. And she did it so delicate-like. That gal could have crocheted a sweater for a hummingbird." I giggle picturing it.

There are merry little pictures of flowers and things. And one . . . I blink. "Hey, that's me!" I pause. "I think. But it looks more like Rory, maybe."

"Neither one of you was around then." Granny gives my shoulder a squeeze. "I'm going to miss you, chicken."

I've been here over a month and have to go back to Bel Air tomorrow.

"I'm going to miss you too, Granny."

I look down at my cowboy boots. I don't want her to see my eyes with their wet twinkles.

For dinner I eat four pieces of corn on the cob and a pile of tomatoes, all from Granny's garden. We don't eat Granny's chickens. They're just for laying eggs. For dessert Granny makes us tin roof sundaes: vanilla ice cream, chocolate sauce, and peanuts on top.

"The ice cream and the peanuts count for protein," Granny says.

While we eat dessert, we turn on the television and Rory's face fills the screen. She's on a pirate ship rescuing some kids who were kidnapped because the pirates thought they could help them find a buried treasure. While balancing on the rail of the ship, Rory is swinging and jabbing with her sword. She snips the buttons off the pirate's waistcoat and then his britches, which fall down, leaving him in his underwear.

Rory does stuff I could never do. She makes Robin Hood look clumsy with a bow and arrow. She always hits the bull's-eye. I squint at her. Something seems a little off about Rory. Maybe it's the reception. Granny puts her glasses on and leans closer. "She looks different, Ryder. A little older." She grabs my hand and gives it a tight squeeze, then tucks it under her arm as if she's scared I might skedaddle. She turns to me. Her pale blue eyes are wobbly behind the magnification of the lenses. "Love ya, chicken."

When I get in bed, I text Penny. *Can you get the Rory show in London? Take a look. Is anything weird about her?*

I wonder if she'll text me back. She never calls anymore and only sometimes answers my text messages.

At about two in the morning, a little ping wakes me up. Penny!

Hi, Ryder. I'm off to a garden party today. Guess who's going to be there? A royal princess!

I text back: *Did you read my text about Rory? Do they have the show there?*

Then she texts: *No idea about Rory or show. Mum's letting me wear heels today! Talk later.*

Mum? Heels? What's with Penny?

CHAPTER 2

Glitter Bombing and
Other Unnatural Disasters

When Dad meets me at the luggage carousel, I know something has changed. As he walks, he literally bounces. And the sad lines around his mouth are gone. We run to hug each other.

"Look at you! Nice and tan. Hope you wore your sunblock. Your nose is peeling a bit."

My face is one big freckle now. Sunblock or not, I get a gazillion freckles.

As soon as we get in the car, he starts talking. It's as if he is talking around something. I listen hard.

"Sweetie, the first thing we're doing is going to Bingo Electronics and I want you to pick out whatever television you want. And before I forget, Penny called from

London the other day. She thought you were back. She's such a great kid."

She wears heels, I want to say. *And gabs about princesses.* But I keep my mouth shut.

"We talked for a while. Would you like to go to London for Thanksgiving?"

"You mean us?"

"No, I mean you. You and Penny could have a blast. Girl time."

Girl time? Dad never talked like this before.

"What about you? And Granny? She'd be all alone."

"Uh . . ." He seems stumped. Then he says, "You know, Bernice has three daughters."

I'm having trouble following him. "Bernice the Radiance lady?"

"Yeah, Bernice. Um . . . you know, she's a movie producer too. And her daughters are nice girls. I hope you like them."

"Why should I like Bernice and her daughters?"

"Well, because I do. . . ."

I am stunned. He told me about her in Deadwood, but if Dad's bringing her up again . . . I have the most horrible thought. Is he in love with Bernice? Is that why I should like her? I look at him out of the corner of my eye. What is he thinking? I feel as if I'm being hit over the head with a sledgehammer right here in the middle of the Los Angeles freeway. There is a long silence. Finally Dad breaks it.

"You're really going to like her. But she's not like Mom."

"Mom was unique," I mutter.

"That she was!" He nods vigorously. "That she was. No one ever like her. Nor will there ever be anyone like her. . . . She . . . she had uniquitude."

Girl time and now *uniquitude! Dad, what has happened to you?*

"It's different than with your mom. That was . . . everything. With Bernice, it's companionship."

Companionship? Is he saying he doesn't love her? I'm too scared to ask. He must be reading my mind, because he says, "Are you thinking I've fallen in love with Bernice, Ryder?"

"I don't know what I'm thinking, Dad."

"Don't worry, sweetie. With Bernice it's, uh . . . We are in *like*. Companionship. Ryder, I've been so lonely. I feel better with a companion."

"I'm a companion."

"You are, and a very good one, but you're my daughter. The best daughter in the world! But I'm talking about . . . grown-up companionship." If he says that word "companionship" one more time, I might throw up.

"I think you're going to like Bernice and her daughters. They're a little bit older than you. Bliss, Joy, and Connie, which is short for Contentment."

"What? Is this like Donald Duck and his nephews Huey, Dewey, and Louie?"

"Don't be sarcastic, Ryder. Please just calm down."

Me calm down? I stare at this man who looks like my dad but who doesn't talk, think, or act like Dad. Maybe aliens have taken him over. I start to get an idea for a new show: *Robot Dad*!

Dad says, "And after checking out the new TVs, we'll go to Sugar Babe to find you a dress for the party."

"What party?"

"A party Bernice and I are giving."

"Sugar Babe!" I screech. "Mom hated that store. How could you?"

"But they have a tween department now. They didn't use to."

Tween is such a weird word—it's like you're nothing. Like a blob of Silly Putty, which in my mind is not that silly or even really putty. I try not to glare. "Look. No Sugar Babe, not the tween, teen, or old ladies' department."

Dad looks at me. He chuckles. "Oh, you're such a card, Ryder!"

I am not a card! I want to scream at him. I remember Dad pretending to pop open his head and put his brain on my nightstand. But maybe Dad didn't misplace his brain. Maybe he had a brain transplant instead.

Revolting . . . disgusting . . . vomititious. But if you vomited when shopping at Sugar Babe, you'd throw up glitter. A lady in a sparkly miniskirt greets us.

"Mr. Holmsby!" she says. "Welcome to Sugar Babe."

"You must be Lorraine."

"I am! Bernice and I were college roommates."

Bernice's college? I think. *Where'd they go? Glitter U?* Then she turns to me.

"And you must be the famous Ryder?"

"Famous?" I say weakly. Dad flashes Lorraine a sharp look.

"Oops!" She slaps her hand over her mouth. "Follow me to Tween!"

Her chemical-blue eyes dart around as if she's looking for muggers to pop out from behind the dress racks. We walk beneath a banner with sparkly words in curly script. *10 Going on 16! Too Old for Toys, Get Ready for Boys.* Pink and red boxes are stacked up on the counters.

"What's that?" I ask.

"Makeup," Lorraine says. "All environmentally friendly. No animal testing."

"Animals hate makeup!" I say. Lorraine doesn't get the joke. But Dad does and tries not to laugh. I love him in that minute. Old Dad is back. But he's nervous.

"Let's get along now. We have other fish to fry," he says.

Fish to fry—that's like something Granny would say. Maybe he's coming back! "Fish? How about a hot dog at Pink's instead?" Pink's makes the best hot dogs.

Dad turns pale as we pass a jewelry counter and

another banner with curlicue writing. *Bling Blast. Let Us Help You Release Your Inner Princess. Coming Soon!* Then I hear what sounds like the theme song from *Super-Rory-Us.*

"We gotta go." Dad grabs my hand and we run out of the store as Lorraine sputters, "But Mr. Holmsby, I had a dress in mind."

When we get back to the car, I look at him. "What just happened?"

"Oh, nothing. But you were right. That place is sort of tacky."

"If I have to get a new dress, I'd rather go to a vintage store. Mom loved those."

"Sure, sweetie."

Why was Dad so weird in the store? I need to think about this. But first—yay!—a hot dog at Pink's.

CHAPTER 3

Home Not-So-Sweet Home

"Ryder! Welcome home!" Bernice comes running out the front door. Behind her troop her daughters: Bliss, Joy, and Connie.

I look at Dad. He's dazed.

The girls totter on platform heels dotted with rhinestones. They could almost be triplets, with the same perfectly long, straight dark hair. Bliss and Joy have bright blue eyes, and Connie, the youngest, has black. Connie's face is heart-shaped, not as thin as her sisters'. They share a blank smile and I give them a name: the Three Happys.

Bernice's hair is yellow with orange tips and stands straight up like a burning haystack. Her face looks like

she's wearing a mask. She must've had so much Botox and other stuff done to her face that it's made her eyebrows and forehead look kind of frozen. But it seems as if she's trying to smile at me, and maybe doing that hurts. I guess that's nice of her. I smile back.

She leaves the facial expressions to her daughters. And right now there's a collective eyebrow raise from the Three Happys. But Mom always said, "You can't judge a book by its cover." Maybe underneath, Bernice and her daughters are wonderful people. As I look from them to Dad, I start to wonder, *Could it be? Are they all cartoons?* I take another look at my sweet and tired Dad. I know I have to try to be nice for him, even if they are cartoons. I grew up with cartoons. I love Rory. And I'm not a cartoon. I'm real.

Bliss smiles. "So happy to meet you, Ryder. What's in your bag?"

Dad says, "We went to a special thrift store that Ryder and her mom loved."

Bernice says, "You went to a thrift store for our party that I have done all the planning for, Ralph?"

Uh-oh.

Dad says, "Why don't you let Ryder put on the outfit so you can see it before you go home?" *Go home!* The two words are music to my ears. "It's really lovely, and it suits her." He sounds like my usual dad. He's back! My heart skips a beat.

Bernice realizes she has gone too far. "All right. I am very open-minded. I am going to meditate and cleanse my SPs."

"SPs?" I ask.

"Spirit points, sweetie," Dad says.

"It's all about spiritual hygiene." Bernice sticks out her very long tongue and licks her cosmetically enhanced lips.

Dad steps close to me. "Learning about my spirit points has helped me so much, Ryder. Helped me to recover."

"Recover?" My voice quavers. I step closer and whisper, "I don't believe you have recovered, Dad." Dad steps back, bewildered.

I see what my mission is: rescue Dad, bring him back to reality. I won't take this cartoon version of my dad. I want the Real Ralph Holmsby.

Dad blinks. "Ryder, Bernice is the codirector of the Inner Radiance Meditation Center. The center has rescued me." He talks like he's a lost dog that's been picked up by animal rescue.

Bernice slips her arm through Dad's. She looks at him with what could be real concern. "Ryder, nobody should have to hurt forever and ever. It was taking a toll on him." She sighs. "You see, dear"—I wince at "dear"—"his spirit points were weakened, battered."

"What exactly are spirit points?" I ask.

"Spirit points are crossroads of nerves, veins, and arteries in the body. They are the centers of life forces. Your dad's spiritual hygiene was in chaos." I think her little speech is *creeeepy*! She's talking like he needed a stronger deodorant. "And now my hygiene needs a bit of attention."

"You don't smell at all," I reply sweetly.

She looks shocked. "As I said a minute ago, I am going to meditate."

Dad gives Bernice a hug. "While you're meditating, dear, Ryder can put on her outfit and you'll see how nice she looks."

Bernice glides away and the Three Happys follow, giggling. But I catch Connie glancing back at me. She's *not* giggling. There's a flicker in her black eyes. It reminds me of that split second Rory looked out from the television screen when she reversed the spell on the owl—an unscripted moment. Curious!

Joy gives her sister a yank. "Connie, don't do your mopey thing."

Mopey? I'm not the only one? Very curious!

I go to my room and get dressed. I don't care much about clothes except for parties. The rest of the time, I just wear jeans or cutoffs. But I absolutely love this outfit. It's a soft-pink antique lace skirt. It's a little big on me, but I have a really cool maroon cummerbund that will keep it up like a belt. For a blouse, I found a white top with buttons that are different shapes. A final touch—brand-new Doc Martens lace-up boots with pink and red roses! Oh, nearly forgot. I am also going to wear a pink beret my mom made for me that has a few feathers from a white cochin, a gorgeous chicken. In a way, this outfit is sort of like Mom's quilt—a crazy patchwork of neat stuff.

I stand in front of the full-length mirror. Behind me is a wireframe statuette of Rory—a Mimi. Wireframe is the first stage of an animated figure, kind of like the skeleton. A Mimi is the big award for film animation. Side by side we look nice in the mirror. We fit together.

Looking at Rory's wireframe, I think maybe everyone has a secret inside self. Maybe even the Three Happys. We aren't supposed to judge a book by its cover. I wonder what the Three Happys and Bernice would look like as a wireframe. Maybe completely different without all that makeup. I'll try to look deeper. I have to try for Dad's sake. And Bernice did try to smile at me even though it must have hurt.

I go out to the pool, where Bernice and the Three Happys are sitting.

"Here I am!" I say cheerfully. Dad beams at me. Bernice is trying to smile again.

"Granny!" Bliss gasps, looking at my outfit. Joy is laughing. Connie just stares. No hint of the flicker I saw earlier.

Dad stands up and glares at them. My chin begins to tremble. *I will not cry. I will not cry.* I take a step forward and stand right in front of Bliss in her metallic shorts and crop top with SEXY BABE in rhinestones on the front. All from Sugar Babe! I take a deep breath and squint. Her inner self, her wireframe, must be in there somewhere.

Nothing.

"If you mean my granny, I am proud to look like her," I say, then turn around.

"Hey, kiddo." My dad reaches out and touches my shoulder. I can see tears in his eyes, but I shrug off his hand. *How can he be doing this to us?*

My dad is really mad. He makes each of the Three Happys write me an apology, which they slip under my door before they go home. Joy and Bliss say basically the same thing. *Sorry to have offended you,* blah, blah, blah. Connie writes something a little different.

Dear Ryder,

I'm sorry we made you sad. I guess you don't need any more sadness. I'm so sorry about your mom. I feel sad sometimes too. After my dad and mom divorced, I was supposed to be with him at least half the time. But he's a scientist and had to go on a sort of secret expedition and now I'm stuck with Mom and my half sisters. Sometimes I wish I could just—I know it sounds stupid—fly off like a bird or something—and find him. Anyhow, sorry how they laughed at your outfit. It was just different. We're not very good with different.

Connie

P.S. My name is Contentment but I secretly think of myself as Constance.

There are a lot of interesting things about this note. First, the sentence *We're not very good with different.* So why is your mom hanging around my dad? He's different from Bernice. But the P.S. is even more intriguing. Does Connie have a secret self buried deep inside her? Is this a glimpse of her wireframe?

I call Penny. I've tried twice since I got home, but she's always out. . . . The phone rings and rings and rings.

"Hello?"

"Penny, I've been trying to get you forever. I miss you!"

"I miss you too! Oh, I know we are out so much. Sorry." Something has changed in her voice. Is she getting a British accent? "Oh, by the way, everyone calls me Penelope here."

"Uh, should I call you that too?"

"Actually, I think I do prefer it. It's so British. But listen, I'm in a terrible rush. Mummy and I are . . ."

Her mom is "Mummy"? I feel as if the whole world is sliding away from me. Everything is changing. My dad, my best friend. I feel sort of like an orphan, or maybe I am an alien in a world I just don't get. I need to call Granny. She'll tell me what to do.

CHAPTER 4

A Phone Call to Granny

Granny picks up on the fifth ring.

"Hello? . . . Oh, now you hush, dollin'. Not you, Ryder. The chicken, Miss Mallow."

I hear a squawk. The phone drops to the ground. I have been through this before with Granny. She never just talks on the phone. She's either knitting or cooking or, in this case, dealing with a nervous chicken.

"Storm coming?" I know storms upset birds.

"You betcha. Miss Mallow here has her knickers in a twist. But we're just going to sit in the rocker here with her on my lap and she'll calm right down."

I'm wishing I could curl up on Granny's lap. So I come right out with it.

"Granny, I've got a problem."

"What kind of a problem?"

"A Bernice kind of a problem, Granny."

"You mean that lady friend of your dad's? He mentioned her in his last phone call. Hoped you'd like her."

"Yes. I think . . ." I can hardly say the words. There's silence on the other end of the phone.

Then, "Oh, dollin'."

"He wants me to like her so much, and her three daughters, who I can't stand. Well, one might be okay. But oh, Granny—" My voice cracks. More silence. I can hear Miss Mallow, the chicken, breathing. "Granny, please don't say I'll get used to her or I'll adjust."

"Why would I say 'you'll adjust'? You're not a car that needs a tune-up. Does your dad say he's in love with her?"

"No. He says he's in like with her. He needs companionship."

"Really?" she murmurs. She takes a deep breath— Granny, not the chicken. "Look, Ryder, there is something he might dare not say or maybe he doesn't even realize it. But the truth is that it might be too painful for him to fall in love or even in like with someone too much like your mom. It is almost as if he's let himself be drawn to someone just the opposite, for your mother was beyond compare. And maybe he thinks it would be an insult to her memory to turn to a woman who is just a dim imitation of Andrea Ryder, one of the most creative, loving women to ever grace our planet."

"Yeah, maybe. But it's so hard, Granny."

"I know, chicken, I know."

I believe she does know. But there isn't much else to say. I'm not going to adjust. I'm not going to get used to anything. I guess I need to hope. What I really need is magic. I need a major Rory-shazam moment!

CHAPTER 5

....

The Invisible Shrinking Me

I've been thinking about what Granny said for days. But the Three Happys barely say a word to me when they are here. Connie hardly speaks to her mom or her sisters. So I guess I shouldn't be offended. The silence is actually rather peaceful. Peaceful, but lonely.

By the time the party rolls around, I feel like a ghost in my own house. I'm being erased bit by bit.

"Oh, sorry! So sorry!" I say to a waiter who nearly knocked me down with a platter of glasses.

"Yikes, sorry!" I say to a man carrying a flower arrangement. He couldn't see me through the roses.

"Whoops, my fault." I step out of the way of another waiter. I'm an epic apologizer. In less than five minutes I have apologized eight times to people I don't even know. I've become a speed bump in my own house.

As I go through the kitchen, I peek into the home theater, which has been commandeered by Bernice. She has installed two makeup artists who are applying industrial-strength false eyelashes to the Three Happys. One of the makeup people sees me.

"Is she going to be made up for the party?"

The Three Happys turn and look at me. "No!" they all say. Then Joy narrows her eyes.

"Hey, you! Did you use my brush?"

"No," I say. "Why would I do that?"

"Well, somebody did who has your hair color."

Bliss turns to the makeup artist. "Can you put another layer of lashes on me?"

She! Hey, you. I am now officially a pronoun. Would it have killed them to say my name? I already checked the dinner tables. No place card for me. Zip. Zilch. I always thought being invisible would be cool, but not this way.

As I leave the makeup room, I take two cocktail weenies from a waitress's tray and pop them in my mouth. The waitress doesn't even notice. She turns and yells, "Hey, where's the tofu platter?" Tofu must have been Bernice's idea. Dad's more of a cocktail weenie type. He and I can plow through two or three dozen easily. Another woman walks by, carrying a platter of mini quiches and mini hamburgers. Who's coming to this party? Munchkins?

CHAPTER 6

Shazam!!!

I skip out on the party early. Cassie Simon, the art director at Starlight Studios, watches me sneak out and looks sadder than she did at my birthday party. Sheldon Weckstein, Dad's lawyer and my friend Eli's father, looks queasy. Eli looks confused.

Before I head upstairs to my room, I stock up on all the party goodies still left in the kitchen, dodging the obstacle course of health food: tofu kabobs, kale chips, and kale dip? Double yuck.

"What, no kale?" someone pipes up behind me. Connie's looking at my plate.

"Oh, hi. My mom called kale 'food with an attitude.'"

Connie smiles. A true smile. "Stuck-up food," she

says. "My mom loves kale. She says it's good for your spirit points." She pauses. "Whateverrrr!" We laugh, and her amazing black eyes twinkle at me.

Is Connie actually making fun of her mom? Whoa! "You . . . you took off the false eyelashes."

"Yeah . . . they just aren't me. I kind of feel stupid in them. They were my mom's idea."

"Oh," I say. Poor Connie. My mom never tried to control how I looked. Connie still looks so uncomfortable—the dress, the shoes, the hairstyle. None of it is Connie. It's almost as if she wants to escape her own skin. Molt like a bird.

Back in my bedroom, I take off my Doc Martens, plop on my bed, and turn on my new huge flat-screen 3-D TV that comes down from the ceiling at the touch of a finger. Dad just bought me this TV. It's a bribe so I'll like Bernice and her kids. I put on my 3-D glasses. What do you know is playing? *Super-Rory-Us.*

It's the same episode I saw with Granny in Deadwood, the one with Rory rescuing the kids from the pirates. I lean forward. There is definitely something strange going on with Rory. Suddenly the screen gets squiggly and—"Shazam!" The word explodes in the room.

Who said that? The music in the program has faded. Rory is sitting on the bottom edge of the screen with her legs dangling a few feet above the carpet. My carpet! Not the deck of a ship! I jump up in shock. This wasn't in the script!

"Finally! I thought you'd never notice! Ryder, I need help," she says. I blink. Take off my 3-D glasses, spit on them, rub them with the corner of my comforter, and put them back on.

I blink again. She's still there and she's *not* a cartoon. She is exactly my size. I see the freckle on her thumb. Her nose is different, yes, but she's . . . kind of me? Where do I leave off and she begins? She does not look like a cartoon now. If I touched her hand, I would feel skin. If I squeezed it, I would feel bone. But I'm sort of afraid to do this.

Rory leans in my face. "It's me, Ryder. Yes, I am real. Take off those stupid glasses. You don't need them."

I'm shaking, but do as I'm told. She's carrying a sword and has a crossbow slung across her back. And she can do a lot of damage with her slingshot tucked into her back pocket. "This cannot be happening," I whisper to myself.

"I'm real, Ryder, and I'm in trouble."

"How is this happening?" I feel a surge of happiness. Suddenly I know that I'm not alone but . . . connected.

"Make Magic Happen, Ryder. Does that ring a bell? The motto of Starlight Studios, on everything except maybe the toilet paper."

The phone rings. Who would call right in the middle of Dad and Bernice's party? I look at caller ID. Granny Ryder, of course!

"Hello," I say.

"Ryder, dollin'."

"Oh, Granny, I'm kind of busy." I study Rory. Her skin, her clothes, aren't those cartoony colors at all. More real like mine. Mine are real—duh, I'm human. And so is she. Shazam!!!

"Oh, my stars and garters, I plumb forgot, it's that party!" Granny exclaims.

"It's not that. I'm just in my bedroom and . . ." Rory is now out of the television completely and jumps on the bed. It creaks. She has weight! She might weigh as much as I do. Cartoons don't have weight. Cartoons aren't in real life! She's examining the Rory comforter and the pillows that show her shooting arrows into a starry night.

"Chicken, this will only take a minute, but I'm concerned."

"About what, Granny?"

"Rory." At that moment I feel a poke in my ribs. A real poke from a real finger into my very real ribs.

"See, what did I tell you?" Rory hisses.

"Hush." She can't be real. I grope around for the 3-D glasses.

"It's not going to help," Rory says.

"Ryder, dollin', is someone else there? You sound distracted."

"No, no one here. Just me—ugh!" I gasp as I feel a kick in my shin. A cartoon kicked me. And it hurt!

"How dare you say no one is here!" Rory is a furious shade of red. The same color I turn when I'm upset. Vermilion, Mom called it.

"I'll make this quick," Granny says. "I saw this rather disgusting commercial for a new Rory doll. She looks too grown-up, and they've done something funny with her eyes—like false eyelashes—and she's gotten too skinny in some places and has matured in other places. Maybe you could ask your dad . . ." There's silence. "Are you still there?"

"Uh . . . I guess so. . . . Uh . . . Sure, Granny, I'll—I'll look into it." That's what my dad often says on a business call.

"Okay, you do that. Love ya! Bye-bye, dollin'."

"Bye, Granny." I set the phone down.

I turn slowly toward the girl sitting next to me on the bed. Behind her, the television has frozen and there's a Rory-sized blank in mid–sword fight with the pirates.

"It's stuck," I say.

"No, Ryder, you're stuck," Rory fires back. "The television will go back when I climb back in."

"It's a flat-screen." *Dumb!* I'm not sure why I said this.

"Doesn't matter," Rory says, and sets her mouth in a

firm little line. It's our NE—nonnegotiable expression. "Ryder, I told you, I'm real and I'm in trouble. Until you understand that I'm real, I am not going back into that TV, and I'll haunt you—flat-screen, Blu-ray, DVD, IMAX theater. The new film, *Glo-Rory-Us,* will be at that new Starlight Studios IMAX on Hollywood Boulevard." I can see tears in her eyes. She looks down at the pillow. "They used too much bleach in the wash. Look at this pillowcase. I look all faded and yucky."

"You know about laundry and bleach?" I ask.

"I know about a lot of things, Ryder. I exist!"

I wanted a major shazam moment, and wow, did I get one.

"Yes!" I say. And throw my arms around Rory and hug her tight. Penny may be in London. And Mom may be gone, but I have a little twinkle of her magic back with Rory here. Let the fun begin!

CHAPTER 7

The Reluctant Royal

"Wait! Run that by me one more time. What did you say these things are again?" Rory asks, picking up a midget hamburger.

"Sliders."

"Why do they call them sliders?"

"I have no idea. But what were you saying—something about a coronation?"

She sighs. Her shoulders slump just the way mine do when I'm sad or about to give up on something.

"The coronation is our situation."

Our situation? I think.

"The ticking bomb," she adds. There's something scary about the way she says this. "Your granny was right. They're changing me just in time for the corona-tion at the movie's premiere," she adds miserably.

"You can't be coronated or whatever. You're not royal. You're not a princess. Just the thought is enough to make me barf."

"Barf?" Rory asks.

Hmmm . . . Some words she doesn't know.

"Throw up. Puke. Vomit. Mom did not want you to be a princess, or for you to wear tiaras or any of that. This stinks!"

"I knew you'd understand, Ryder. I just knew it." Rory grabs my hands. Our hands are so much alike. The freckle on our left thumb is how I learned right from left when I was little.

"But why is this happening?" I moan.

"It's all because of the movie. It's a whole different script from the TV shows. I get captured and put in the Witch of Wenham's tower. She's holding me for ransom."

"But you fight your way out, right?"

"Not this time."

"You mean you . . . die?"

"No, the prince rescues me."

"Prince Thunderdolt Lowenbrow? That dope? You're always rescuing him. You gotta be kidding."

"It gets worse."

"How much worse can this get?"

"I marry him."

"You can't be forced to marry him."

Rory shakes her head slowly. "Ryder, it's written in the script. We're animated characters. Made up. We have no control over our lives."

"But this is crazy. Marry the prince? Are they nuts? For crying out loud, you're eleven years old."

"They've kind of sped up my age. In the movie I'm a teenager. They want to appeal to older kids."

"But I just caught up with you. We're eleven! And a teenager is still too young to get married." I remember Dad grumbling over the phone once to someone at Starlight: "Rory is a middle-grade kid. Why do you want her to be older? It doesn't make sense," he said.

"And you know what else? No more weapons. I have to carry a wand. My slingshot is a thing of the past."

"A wand? What the heck are you going to do with a wand? Is it magic?" Rory shakes her head no. "How can you kick butt with a wand that isn't even magic? And here I wanted Dad to upgrade you to an ax. An ax in combo with your slingshot would make you indestructible. Hey, you could wear a dress or a tiara or anything with an ax—I don't care what you wear—but you're not going to be kicking any butt with a wand. But a slingshot plus an ax—elegance, skill, brains, and brawn. A wand! Gimme a break!"

"And wait, the shoes."

"What? I said a dress is okay but boots are a must."

"The boots have rhinestones and spike heels."

"Rory, I know you're good, but you're not doing that sword fight balancing on the pirate ship's rails with spike heels. No way. And if you had an ax, you could have cut the rigging. I mean, without your weapons, how will you ever fight all those thugs in Ecalpon?"

"You're preaching to the choir here, girl! Everything you say is right."

My eyes fly open. "Preaching to the choir" was one of Mom's favorite expressions. It means you're arguing with someone who already agrees with you. Mom. Tears stream down my face.

"I miss her, Rory. I miss her so much."

I don't want to say what I'm thinking, but I sort of wish it had been Mom who stepped out of the television instead of Rory. Maybe heaven has different rules than whatever this is that allows Rory to get out of the television. But I don't need another me. I need Mom.

Rory puts her arm around my shoulder.

"I know, Ryder. I miss her too."

We both sit there for a long time listening to the music from the salsa band outside.

"Are you like my sister, Rory?" I finally ask.

"Sort of."

I know what she means. It's more like we're different versions of each other.

"Do you have any pictures of Mom?" she asks. "I mean Andy."

"You can call her Mom. I mean, she's like your mom, she made you up." She nods. I tell her, "I have this scrapbook where I write things down and draw and have photos of her. Wanna see it?"

"Yes," she says softly.

I get the scrapbook from the shelf above my desk. The first picture is a photograph of Mom in her fifth-grade class at Deadwood Elementary School.

"That's Mom on the far left." I have never shown this to anyone else.

I turn the page to one of my drawings: a truck with this goofy creature that's sort of half dog, half cat.

"Wow, you can really draw just like your mom. That's cool."

I look at her. People don't say "cool" in Ecalpon. Rory is picking up stuff fast.

"Well, you're better with a slingshot. I did this drawing when I was four. That's all I drew for about a year—this creature. I called it a drat, since it was half dog and half cat. I liked having him drive things." I skip forward a few pages.

"That's a beautiful portrait of your mom. Did you draw that too?

"Yep. Two weeks before she died. B-but . . . but," I start stammering. I always do now when I think about drawing.

"But what?"

"I haven't really been able to draw since Mom died. My hand sort of freezes up."

"That's too bad. What's that writing under it?"

"A limerick. My dad and I like to write them. We have contests. So this was his about Mom."

Rory bends over and begins to read it out loud.

> *"There is a lady named Andy*
> *Who is ever so clever and handy.*
> *She has brains galore*
> *And makes a mean s'more.*
> *As a wife and a mom she's a dandy."*

I reach for a pencil and begin to cross some of the words out and put in others.

"What are you doing?" Rory asks.

"Wrong tense."

> *There once was a lady named Andy*
> *Who was ever so clever and dandy.*
> *She had brains galore*
> *And made a mean s'more.*
> *As a wife and a mom she was dandy.*

"Has he written one about Bernice yet?"

"No, but I have." I turn a few pages. She reads it out loud. We're giggling after the second line.

"There is a lady named Bernice
Whose face never shows a crease.
She can't even smile
And is full of guile.
How I wish she would go and decease."

Someone knocks on the door.

"Ryder, dear?" It's Bernice! "Want to open the door?"

I hear a little crackle from the television and turn toward Rory, but she's gone. The frozen frame on the TV has unfrozen. There she is back in Ecalpon, prancing on the rail of the ship and about to do in the pirate. "Say your prayers, Scummy Sam! The sword or the deep?"

What about me? What about my prayers? Rory, come back! I look to the screen. *Help! Help me!* I cry out silently. *Please* Shazam?

The door opens. And there is no magic.

Bernice peers around the door. Dad's behind her. Joy and Bliss grin at me. Their eyeliner looks as if it has been put on with a spatula. The spiky false eyelashes ring their eyes like dark picket fences. I wonder where Connie is. Bernice's tongue—is it forked?—pokes out as she licks her chops—in anticipation? Anticipation of what?

Nausea begins to rise from my gut. My mom and dad always said, "You'll feel better if you just let yourself throw up."

"It's like magic," Mom would say. "You instantly feel better." And she would wave her hand like a vomit fairy godmother.

"I think I'm going to barf."

Dad recognizes the symptoms. "Okay, clear the room!" He rushes in, grabs a wastebasket. Afterward, he helps me to the bathroom to tidy up. Then, into bed. "Now lie back, sweetie."

"Just let me sleep, Dad, just let me sleep." And so I fall into a deep, dreamy, healing sleep.

CHAPTER 8

Back in Make-Believe

"She's back!" I hear Mum call out.

As I trot up the path on Calamity, I can see both Mum and Da rushing out of the cottage. And . . . God's knee-caps! Our servant, Bethilda, is trying to curtsy. She started practicing as soon as she got wind of the script changes and what might happen between me and Prince Thunderbolt. She's tall for an old lady and skinny as a stick. It's painful to watch her try and fold herself into a curtsy.

"You're back. How was it?" Mum asks breathlessly.

Da, who looks a bit nervous, steps up and gives Mum's shoulder a squeeze. "Just think, Gyrfrid, our little girl has been to places we've never seen. She got out of this virtual world, our make-believe world, and into . . . blimey . . . what do they call it?"

"The *real* world, Phinegal. The *real* world," Mum replies as if she is tasting something delicious.

"But we're in Starlight Studios, aren't we, dear?" Da asks.

"Yes, in a computer."

"But we're 3-D, aren't we?" he says.

"If people wear 3-D glasses, Phin." Mum turns to me. "Did the little girl wear them?"

"*Ryder*, Mum, that's her name."

"Well, did Ryder wear 3-D glasses when you came out of that television set?"

"At first. She didn't believe I could be real."

"How did you convince her?"

"I kicked her," I say.

"Kicked her! Oh dear, oh dear!" Bethilda is wringing her hands. "Not proper behavior for a prin—"

"No *P* word!" I shout. "It makes me vomit!"

"Now, now, dear. Calm down," Mum says. "Let me give you some honey mead broth. That always settles the tummy. And I can slip in a leaf of royal mint. It's in bloom."

"Nothing royal, please. I'll barf."

"Whaaat?" Mum, Da, and Bethilda look at me as if am speaking another language.

"Barf, like vomit."

"That is a word? Wherever does it come from?" Da asks.

"Outside. The real world."

"Barf?" My da cocks his head. "It has a certain ring to it. Rather like it, I do. The hound, Bessie, just had pups. There's a big fellow in the litter. I'll call him Barf."

"Call the pup anything you want, but don't call me the *P* word," I mutter.

"Now stop this fussing," Mum says. "Let's go inside and have Rory tell us what the outside world is like. The *real* world."

I begin my tale over mugs of honey mead broth. Mum is fascinated. She keeps repeating "real world" with a strange hush, as if no one is supposed to know about my adventure there. In her mind it is a fantastical place.

"You realize, my dear, that you are a pioneer." Her voice bubbles with admiration. I am her Christopher Columbus, her conquistador who sailed to the distant shores of a New World.

"Pioneer! That's a *P* word." Bethilda gives a cackle as she sets down a jug of cream and a plate of biscuits. I look at Bethilda. I get an odd shivery feeling. What is it about Bethilda that is somehow different yet awfully familiar? She goes back to the woodstove and begins pouring batter into small loaf pans. "I'm making some groat cakes for Calamity. You know how she loves them, dearie. I thought it must have been a hard trip for her. Long ride to that place."

"You mean the *real* world," Mum says brightly, and once more the word "real" seems almost to shimmer in the air.

"That's nice of you, Bethilda," I say, staring at her straight back. She's very fond of Calamity and is always making her special treats. *Something is a tiny bit different about her.* "But I didn't take Calamity all the way, Bethilda."

"Why ever not?" She turns to look at me.

"Well, it would be hard getting her out of the television set and into Ryder's bedroom. And I just didn't want to have any accidents."

"Accidents?" Bethilda says. "What kind of accidents?"

"In the real world, people and animals poop."

Mum's mouth drops open. Da blinks.

"I . . . I . . . thought there might be things we didn't know about in the real world. I mean, it must be so different from our world. But you learned this when you crossed over, I assume?" Da is still blinking.

"I sort of knew about it before. They have special rooms—at least, the people do. And just before I crossed over into Ryder's bedroom, I heard her go into the bathroom."

"And poop?" Mum asks.

"Pee. Then I heard the chamber pot flush."

"Flush? Chamber pots?" Da blinks again.

"Actually, they call them toilets. Not chamber pots."

"And even princesses poop in these . . . these . . . toilets?" Bethilda says in utter disbelief. I nod.

I think I can safely say that no animated character has ever pooped on-screen in television history. If it happens, it's off script.

I suddenly realize why Bethilda looks strangely familiar. I remember the picture in Ryder's room of her granny flashing a big smile on a horse. Now, I have never in all my animated life seen Bethilda on a horse, and she wears a kerchief, not one of those cowboy hats like Ryder's granny. But there has always been that gap in her teeth just like the one in Ryder's granny's teeth. Now it's gone. "Bethilda, what happened to your teeth? No more gap."

"No, dear. I think they did that to me at Starlight Studios somehow. Animators decided to fix my teeth."

"For this movie," Mum says grimly.

"D-don't you miss it, Bethilda?" I stammer.

"Miss what?" she asks.

"The gap in your teeth."

Bethilda's bright brown eyes fix on me. She tips her head to one side. "A gap is a space with nothing. How can I miss nothing?"

"I suppose that's true," I say weakly. "But I liked you

the way you were. And now you can't whistle." *Whistle*, I think, *like Ryder's granny*. How do I know that Ryder's granny whistles when she calls up her horse Calamity from the pasture? I can almost hear it. It's as if on my first trip to the real world I picked up things that I never knew about or heard about before. Maybe because Ryder knows them.

"That's sweet, dear. But you know, things have to change sometimes. I don't mind not whistling. We all have to sacrifice."

"No! No! That's just the point. And things don't have to change." *At least, not in our make-believe, virtual world*. The thought jolts me, but I dare not say it out loud. "I don't want to be what they are making me be."

"A princess?" Bethilda whispers the word.

"I heard that, Bethilda. It's not just that. They are doing weird things to my body." I turn toward my mum and da. "You haven't seen what I have in the *real* world." I try to say "real" just the way Mum always says it, as if it is some sort of super paradise.

"What?" Mum says, tense.

"They're making Cassie draw me taller, with this teensy-weensy waist."

"Oh, Cassie! How I do wish we could talk to her. She's drawn you wearing a corset?" Bethilda asks.

"Sort of. And I'm a lot skinnier."

"What?" Mum is clearly outraged. "We feed you."

"Skinnier? No. Certainly not," booms Da. "You're a strapping girl with muscle, speed, endurance."

"They're making Cassie redraw me for the new movie."

"But why?"

"I have to match all the new products. The dolls, the posters, the live girl actress who will play me in the coronation at the Starlight Studios amusement park."

"Coronation!" Bethilda sighs dreamily.

"And you saw this?" Mum asks, her voice trembling. "In the real world?" The last two words seem to sputter, then collapse, wrinkled like a balloon that has lost its air. "What else did you see, Rory? Aside from the flushing chamber pots," Mum whispers.

Da leans across the table. "Was it like those maps of yore when folk thought the world was flat and the mapmakers would write at the edges of the known world 'Here There Be Dragons'?" His blue eyes sparkle as if catching a glimpse of a distant and unimaginable coastline.

"No dragons in Starlight Studios. When I was by the portal, I could see Cassie's desk. She had samples from the new Rory product line—strange-looking dolls and posters and lunchboxes. The pictures on them sort of looked like me, but not really. My hair was long and silky, not short and curly the way it is now." I sigh wearily. "I have to carry a wand and wear a tiara."

"Tiara! And a wand!" Bethilda claps her hands glee-fully.

I give her a withering look. "Bethilda, you can't kick any butt with a wand."

"Kick butt?" Mum, Da, and Bethilda repeat, con-founded.

"What's that?" Da asks. I know Da is picturing a cute piglet's butt with a curly little tail and me chasing it about the slops trough.

"A real-world term that means 'fight,' Da. Not chasing piglets. Combat."

"Real-world terminology," Da whispers to himself.

"And not only that," I continue. "I'm wearing a very low-cut gown, not my usual tunic. And it has sparkles all over it. My lips are puffy. And my eyes have very thick, long eyelashes and have this stupid look in them."

"They're making you flirt!" Da is seething. "I won't have you flirting. How can you shoot a bow and arrow if you're flirting? How can you win a sword fight if you're batting those lashes?" He looks me straight in the eye. "What else did you see?"

"Cassie." I gulp. "Cassie crying."

"Why was Cassie crying?" Da asks.

"It was so sad. She buried her head in her arms and was sobbing, 'They can't do this to her . . . they can't. It's so wrong. It's all marketing.'"

"Marketing?" Mum asks. "Like going to the

Coddington market when we take the spring piglets?" Many episodes of *Super-Rory-Us* begin at the Coddington market that is held every Friday in the village square.

"No. It's this stuff. All these products they make—the Rory dolls, the games, the puzzles, the costumes."

"Anyhow, the phone rang and Cassie picked it up. She started yelling, 'Andy Holmsby did not create Rory to be a princess! That was the last thing in the world she wanted. She wanted a girl who is strong and brave, who is outspoken and fights for what is right and doesn't give a hoot about some brainless Prince Charming.' Then she slammed the phone down and said some bad words."

Mum shakes her head. "That's not G-rated at all."

"Mum, I was in the real world. People say and do all sorts of un-G-rated things."

Her jaw begins to tremble and she dabs her eyes. "Start at the beginning, Rory, and tell us everything you saw in this so-called real world." Mum's nose wrinkles slightly, as if she is smelling something bad.

"It wasn't as hard as I thought it might be getting across. First I just had to slip through the portal into the streaming-on-demand mode. Before I knew it, I was in the streaming content. That was the hard part. I kept popping up in the wrong programs. I don't think anybody saw me. But then I found the way into the stream that took me directly to what Ryder was watching, and when I felt the time was right, I just stepped out and—Shazam!"

"Just stepped out? Like magic!" Mum's and Da's voices are filled with wonder. "Shazam indeed!" Da exclaims.

"I think it was a little bit of magic. You see, I think there are these places where the borders of the make-believe world and the real world bump up against each other and that's where I was able to come out, slip through the layers like a leak. But the big question is, will it be possible for Ryder to come to our world so she can help me? I think that is the only chance I've got to fix this problem. But first I have to go to sleep. Let me tell you, the real world can tire you out."

I crawl up to the little loft space where I sleep on a mattress made of sweet grass and petals from spring flowers. Mum tucks me in, gives me a kiss, and leaves. There is a little round window. I can see the moon and the stars. Andy Holmsby knew a lot about stars, and she insisted on the proper constellations being painted for the right season. It is the end of summer, and I can see the Cygnus the Swan swooping up into the night. There are all sorts of stars powdering the computer-generated indigo sky, but the constellations really seem to shimmer. I know that the star in the tail of the swan is called Deneb. Ryder was surprised that I knew about laundry bleach; I wonder what she'll think when I tell her I know all about astronomy.

I know more than I've told Ryder. When I climbed back into the television set at Ryder's house, I didn't just go straight home. I think of streaming like a river, an electronic river full of TV shows. So I jumped back in and found my way into the television monitor in the home theater in Ryder's house.

The makeup people were packing up little suitcases with their bottles and tubes and other stuff, and boy oh boy oh boy! What I heard there about Bernice's daughter Bliss!

One makeup artist said, "Bliss doesn't look a thing like Rory, but with the movie changes it might be easier."

Why were they trying to make Bliss look like Rory? God's kneecaps! It can mean only one thing: Bliss will be playing the newly crowned Princess Rory at the movie premiere coronation! As I fall asleep, I remember Cassie's exact words to another animator: "You know, Bernice was once a TV producer, and she's dying to be a part of *Super-Rory-Us* in any way she can."

This is going to knock Ryder's socks off. The perfect place for Bernice to get involved with *Super-Rory-Us* is to have Bliss be the "princess" for the coronation. The thought almost makes me nauseous, but hey, I'm in make-believe territory. A no-barf zone.

BETHILDA

CHAPTER 9

Forever Seventy-One

At the end of the day, Bethilda goes to her small quarters near the chicken house. The soft cluckings of the chickens are comforting, and she often soothes them in return, especially during thunderstorms. But tonight Bethilda is the one in need of soothing. She is deeply confused. She knows that her mistress Gyrfrid is right—that Rory was "created" as an eleven-year-old and she, Bethilda of Saxby-on-the-Weston, was created as a seventy-one-year-old lady. But Bethilda is more and more confused as she hears her masters and Rory talking about this real world.

How did Rory get across? Bethilda doesn't quite understand all this portal and streaming business. Rory must have crossed over while off script. Bethilda likes when they are off script, the way they all were when they weren't in the show but talking as a family around the table. Everyone could say what they thought. Bethilda had thought that being a princess, being royal, would have been thrilling to Rory. She certainly would have been thrilled when she was a little girl to become a . . . Bethilda stopped.

"Stupid me," she mutters. "I've never been a little girl. I have always been seventy-one years old." *I will never be seventy-two. Or eighty, or sixteen. I have never had young years when I might have actually been pretty.* She peers into a small mirror that hangs on a hook above her tin washbasin. Her face is creased with deep lines. The wrinkles were created by the deft sketching hand of Andy Holmsby. The old lady's face was further perfected and scanned into that computer thing. Bethilda has lost track of how they transformed her into a character from that point on. She leans in closer. The gap between her teeth is certainly gone. "I believe they really are getting me ready for service to a princess!"

She sighs. *Why does Rory have to be so goldarn stubborn? "Goldarn"—where did that word come from?* Sometimes words and thoughts just pop up. She supposes it's just part of getting old. *No! You fool. You are old. Always have been!* She glances at the Bible by her bed. She imagines that it is not really proper to pray for someone to become a princess. Well, she must prepare herself to consign the idea of Rory being royalty to that slag heap of dreams out in the Valley of Deletions, just north of the East Grief Road. That is where all the ideas, sketches, and scans that don't work for the show go. An animation dump. She could probably find her tooth gap out there somewhere. But how does one look for nothing—a gap? She smiles at herself in the mirror. She looks so much better now.

CHAPTER 10

· · · · · · · · · · · · · · · · ·

Crossing to Make-Believe

I'm half asleep, but I can't stop thinking about what happened before the visit from the vomit fairy godmother. Bernice and two of the Three Happys were peeking around my bedroom door. An invasion. But before that, Rory, real Rory, was climbing out of the TV set. It all seemed so real. I want it to be real. I don't want it to be a dream, even if it was just a good dream.

I text Penny—sorry, Penelope.

Pen—you'll never believe what happened!!!

I lie back down and wait for the little bing. Nothing.

I'm a little . . . uh . . . misty, as if I'm not quite real, as if I'm somehow floating. I think I'm in my bed. But maybe I'm not. The TV is still on, but it's a different show.

I climb out of bed and glance at the sheets. Rory's words come back to me: *Too much bleach. Look at this pillowcase. I look all faded and yucky.* She *was* here. She knows about bleach. *But not sliders.* "And I know about stars," a voice in my head seems to say.

One thing I know is, Rory needs all the help she can get and so do I. I look at my cell phone. No sign of Penelope. I turn toward the TV and step closer.

"You're here . . . you're close . . . this really happened," I whisper. The television seems to go nuts as the screen turns super squiggly. Where am I? Shazam!

"You're here!" A figure steps out of a little stone cottage with a thatched roof. A shaft of moonlight illuminates her path across the dewy grass.

"Rory!"

"You did it. You crossed over."

"I'm in Ecalpon?" I catch my breath. It is beautiful. The night shimmers with stars. The grass is pearled with dew. A harvest moon floats low on the horizon. White night-blooming flowers tip their faces toward the sky, opening their petals to the darkness, while the morning glories have folded up and wait for dawn. Everything seems more real than real. The air stirs with the fragrance of hay, mud, chopped wood, and smoke. I am tottering on a fine edge between disbelief and belief. I look at my hands and arms. It seems as if my skin is a little pinker, less tan.

"Do I have a bunch of freckles on my face? Is my nose still peeling?"

"Nope!"

"How come?"

"Things are kind of perfect here. You're an animated figure now. Besides the missing freckles, you also don't have . . ." Rory hesitates. "Bones."

"Good grief!" I squeeze my wrist. My fingers just sort of pass through it. "But how did this happen?"

"I'm not sure. Does it matter?" Rory asks.

"Is . . . is this like . . . uh, Peter Pan and believing in fairies when Tinker Bell was—"

"Her!" Rory nearly explodes. "Do you see any wings around here?" She pats her shoulders. "Honestly, Ryder."

This virtual world is a lovely place. I look up and see the stars.

"That's Cygnus the Swan. The star in the end of its tail is Deneb. I know a lot about stars," Rory says.

"I know you do," I reply. "I don't see many stars because of the smog in Los Angeles."

"Smog? Is it kind of like barf?"

I scratch my head. "I never thought of it that way. But yeah! Air barf. It's dirty air from cars and factory pollution."

"Maybe 'smarf' is a better word," Rory says, and we both laugh.

"There's no smog in Deadwood, and when I visit Granny we go up on her roof and look at the stars."

"Oh, lovely!"

"But so is this. This is really lovely," I say, gazing up at the sky.

"Your mum painted every one of those stars, Ryder. She was very particular about the stars."

"I know," I say softly. It feels sort of strange, but I'm beginning to realize that Rory knows almost as much about Mom as I do. Of course, when I was in day care or school, Mom was at Starlight Studios working on Rory. Rory had Mom during the day. Yikes, she might have even spent more time with my mom than I did. Should I feel . . . jealous? Nope. I just want to see this place that Mom created and went to every day. I want to see Ecalpon!

"Can you show me around? This is so cool. These stars and the house. Where is the castle of that dopey prince—Prince Thunderdolt Lowenbrow? Comic relief, Mom always said. That's why she invented him for the series. She said every story needs a fool as much as a villain."

"Hmmm . . . that is probably true." I can tell Rory is a little bit uncomfortable with what I just said. I worry that I've insulted her somehow.

"No offense," I say quickly.

"Oh, no, none taken." But I can see that something is troubling her.

"Rory? What's wrong?"

"Ryder, there are a couple of things you have to understand."

"Sure. Tell me."

"Well, no one could see me or hear me when I came to you in the real world. But I think that it's not going to be the same for you here. You've become sort of one of us. You've become a character."

Character. It's a bit like trying on a new set of clothes or maybe even a new body. I have to think about it for a minute, or maybe two minutes. Rory is patient.

"But, Rory, when you crossed over to my world, you became a human and no one could see you except me. Right?"

"Yes. But believe me, they will see you here."

"How do you know that?"

"Because you . . . *you,* Ryder Eloise Holmsby, are the inspiration for *me* and the entire show. They're going to recognize you. It's not a secret here. And people here will be able to see you and hear you, and know that you're the original and the source of our world."

I'm trying my best to understand. It's a huge idea. She takes a step closer.

"Ryder, what the animators create they see in their

imaginations. They design it, draw it, and enter it all into the computer. But at the same time, they can't imagine these characters ever becoming real. They might just throw up their hands and their pens and their brushes—and computer tools—and say to themselves, 'If the character is real, then I am just a reporter, not an artist.' Animators like Cassie Simon are artists, and all the rest who work on the series and the movie would think they were less creative if I actually existed outside of Ecalpon. Only the inspiration gets to exist in the so-called real world. Not the make-believe character. The door is shut to us."

"But you opened that door. That's strange. It's all strange," I say.

"That's the truth. And truth is stranger than fiction, at least the fiction that the animators make up." I look at Rory and think, *She knows so much, including famous sayings like "Truth is stranger than fiction."*

"Okay, okay," I say slowly. "I understand. I'll behave myself when you introduce me to your parents and all."

"Oh, you don't need to behave yourself that much." She pauses and her eyes crinkle up just the way mine do when I think of something funny. "If you behave too well, they won't believe you're me."

Confusing? My head is spinning.

THE WITCH OF WENHAM

CHAPTER 11

Script Sick

The countryside is bright with the silvery light of the risen moon, and the Witch of Wenham is peering through her telescope. "Two," she mutters. "Two of those despicable little girls!" She addresses a lizard and narrows her yellowish eyes. "How do you explain it, Jeeves?" The lizard Jeeves is an ugly creature about the size of a cat. He purrs like a cat as well. His incandescent eyes flash periodically, revealing a peculiar blue vertical slit.

"Cat got your tongue?" She licks her lips, and Jeeves notices, perhaps for the first time, that her tongue is exceedingly long for a human character. His is long— but he's a reptile. "Mind that tongue, Jeeves, or I might trade you in for a vampire bat. Always fancied one—a can-do kind of butler. Not like you. One that can fly, you know."

"Indeed, madam."

"But back to these vile little girls. What is the meaning of all this? How did this one cross over?"

"I can't explain it, madam. It's definitely off script."

"Off script, on script, I'm sick of scripts. I thought I was supposed to be able to turn that dratted owl into gold."

"Yes, madam. But they rewrite the scripts all the time. In the real world it's a crime against the environment to kill an owl."

"I was just turning it into gold."

"Perhaps a toad would have better suited."

"Toads? No thanks." She snorts. "Why don't I get to do anything I want to do?"

Jeeves groans. "We don't have a choice, no free will, madam." He has explained this a thousand times.

"I don't believe that, Jeeves! Rory chose to cross over, and now this little creep, the original, has crossed back. If that's not free will, what is?"

The lizard is stumped.

"Jeeves!" the witch snaps. "Do what you do best."

"And what is that, madam?"

"Slither! You are my eyes and ears. My spy. Find out all you can. Those girls are up to no good. I think they're trying to change the script."

"Well, that might be good. No one seems very happy with these new developments. Rory's engagement to the prince and all that."

"No one?" A bristly eyebrow hikes up toward a wart on the witch's forehead.

"Uh, maybe Bethilda. She always liked the idea of serving a princess."

"Just Bethilda?" the witch says. "You foolish reptile. I like the script. I have dreams too."

"What dreams, madam?"

"For Byogen."

"Your daughter, Byogen."

"You know what 'Byogen' means in the old language of Ecalpon?"

"Bliss," Jeeves says softly.

RORY

CHAPTER 12

A Mysterious Gap

I can tell Ryder is confused. And of course I'm really nervous because I haven't told her yet about the plans for Bliss to be crowned princess at Starlight Land, the Starlight Studios amusement park, at the premiere of *Glo-Rory-Us*. I'm afraid she'll have a heart attack. Luckily, I can delay breaking the news. Ryder really wants a tour of Ecalpon.

The stars are beginning to fade and dawn is breaking when we start off. On the path to the barnyard, we see Bethilda with her wicker basket, going to collect eggs from the chicken house.

"Oh, look, Bethilda!" Ryder whispers. "Bethilda the servant, right?

"Yeah." I'm wondering if she'll see the resemblance

to Granny. I'm also praying that Bethilda doesn't see us and start to curtsy. I whisper to Ryder, "You know, Bethilda is a compulsive curtsyer."

"No kidding. I wonder why?"

"Who knows?"

"Oh my goodness!" Bethilda says, and starts to curtsy. I'm standing behind Ryder and I shake my head and mouth *No!* at Bethilda. She sees, makes a very good recovery and tips her bonnet at us instead. "I cannot tell you how pleased I am to finally meet you, Ryder. The inspiration! I can't quite believe you came. Was it a hard crossing, dear?"

"No, not really," Ryder replies.

"Well now," Bethilda says. "I must run along to the chicken coop and get the eggs while they are nice and warm. Nothing like a fresh, warm egg."

"Bye," Ryder says. "So nice to meet you."

"Nice to meet you," Bethilda says, and trots off.

"Why are you looking at me that way, Rory?"

"Oh, no reason," I say. I can't believe she doesn't notice Bethilda's resemblance to her granny. "Does she remind you of anybody?"

"No, not in the least."

"Do you remember that she had a gap in her teeth before?"

"Did she? Oh, yes. Now that you mention it, I do. Guess she got her teeth fixed."

"Guess so," I reply vaguely, but I can't help thinking

that there's a mysterious "gap" in Ryder's eyes. Why can't she see the similarity between Bethilda and Granny Ryder? I have only seen pictures of Granny Ryder, and I can see it!

"Oh, you know who I'd love to see?" Ryder says.

"Who?"

"Calamity!"

"The horse?" This is hopeful. Maybe she does see the resemblance and that's what made her think of Calamity.

But then she says, "You have to ride Calamity, since there isn't a Granny character. I mean, how could there ever be another Granny!"

I want to say, *Well, there is another you, and it's me.* But I don't.

Mum and Da are already out and on their way to the Coddington market with the new batch of piglets. Ryder can meet them later. "I'll introduce you to the neighbors."

"I'd love to meet that dopey Prince Thunderdolt Lowenbrow."

"Okay, let's go!"

Sooner or later I'm going to have to tell her about Bliss and the coronation. But for now I welcome any delay— even a visit to Prince Thunderdolt Lowenbrow.

CHAPTER 13

The Glower in the Tower

Just before we reach the castle, a barn owl swoops down and perches on my shoulder.

"Cool," Ryder says. "It's the owl the Witch of Wenham tried to turn into gold! You rescued her!"

"Yes, she is very grateful."

"She should be! Do you think she would perch on me?" Ryder says.

"Offer her your arm and we'll see," I tell her. Ryder sticks out her arm. The owl immediately hops onto it and climbs to her shoulder. Ryder turns around to look at the bird, and they seem to lock gazes for just a second. I can see something clicking in Ryder's brain. The owl flies off and Ryder tips her head, watching, until the owl is swallowed by the night.

"She's so pretty! Wish she'd hung around," Ryder says.

"Well, you know, she was only in that one episode. Probably production is short on sketches for her."

When we get to the castle gates, the guard comes out and says, "I wouldn't advise interrupting him, Your . . ." *Don't say it!* I think. The *H* word, as in "Highness." It hasn't happened yet. I grab Ryder's hand and we rush past the guard and a footman about to bow, and then a scullery maid collapses in an awkward curtsy. Oh dear, is there such a malady as Knee-Jerk Curtsy Syndrome? Every palace servant we pass is ready to bow, scrape, and curtsy as Ryder and I go by.

"I would like to see the prince, please," I say to his personal steward, Hendrik, who seems slightly alarmed by the two of us.

"And this is?" he whispers, and cocks his head with an expression of near disbelief. Then he coughs slightly, almost apologetically. "For security measures, might I see her"—he drops his voice—"TM?"

"What?" shrieks Ryder. "This is worse than airport security. TM? What's that? I'm not carrying liquids, metal, or—"

"Calm down," I say.

"What the heck is a TM?"

"Trademark," I answer.

"But I'm the real thing."

"The real thing!" Hendrik repeats. His voice quavers, as if he has just stumbled into a horror movie.

"Yes, the inspiration. Now please let us through."

"Let me warn you the prince is in the Glower Tower."

"Again?" I say. "What is it now?"

"I'd rather not say." Hendrik looks embarrassed.

We walk up the spiraling staircase of the east tower. Halfway up I start thinking, *Maybe I better begin to tell Ryder about Bliss.* I stop and look at her very seriously.

"Ryder, I have to tell you something."

"Don't worry, I know this prince is not the sharpest blade in the drawer."

"It's not just that."

"What else?"

"Well, with this coronation and me becoming a princess . . ."

"It ain't gonna happen!"

"We can hope. But there's some possibly good news—and then there's bad news."

"Bad news first," Ryder says.

"So you know about the coronation."

"Yep. And if it happens, they're going to have to find someone taller than me, with long, straight hair and a skinny, skinny waist."

"They have, Ryder."

"They have?"

"Who?"

"Bliss," I say.

"Bliss!" she shrieks. Then, in a weak voice, "So what's the good news?"

"I'm not marrying you! That's the good news." Prince Thunderdolt comes blasting out of his tower, wearing a lab coat and holding a test tube. I've never seen him dressed this way. "No way, José. And don't tell me that I have to grow up, like my dad does," the prince blurts out.

Ryder and I look at each other with our eyebrows raised.

CHAPTER 14

· · · · · · · · · · · · · · · · · ·

An Inspiration Unknown

"So this is the Glower Tower?" Rory asks as I look around. No princely trappings at all, but shelves and shelves of books and what looks like a primitive microscope and little glass tubes filled with mysterious liquids. "You're not working with the Witch of Wenham, are you?" Rory asks.

"That quack. Don't be ridiculous. You don't believe in that garbage, do you?" He begins muttering under his breath: "Idiot woman with her charms and spells and little magical cakes. Not science!" There is something about the way he speaks that is vaguely familiar, but it's at odds with the way he looks—chubby and sort of, uh, dare I say Neanderthalish? He has a prominent brow, thus the name Lowenbrow, and buckteeth. Orthodontia desperately needed. But there's a sparkle in his eyes that suggests he's not dumb at all. The sparkle is familiar. Someone I know. Not Penelope, although his eyes are the same color as hers.

He's completely absorbed with orange fluid bubbling in a beaker over a small flame. I wander around.

"Don't touch anything!" he shouts.

"Just looking." Many of the books have titles in curious alphabets.

"What's this?" I point at one ancient tome and turn around. "I can't read the writing. It sort of looks like . . ."

He removes the bubbling beaker from the flame and places it in a bowl of water to cool. He squints at the book and then walks over. "Hebrew," he says. "Duh!"

Duh! Knock me over with a feather! Remove the chubbiness and lift the heavy brow an inch or two and there he is! "You're Eli Weckstein!" I blurt out. "Is this your . . . your Torah portion?"

"Does that look like a Torah to you? No way. It's one of the great Jewish scholar Maimonides's few books on mathematics—conics, to be exact."

"Con-what?" Rory and I say.

"Conics. It's a part of analytic geometry. Deals with three types of cones—hyperbolas, parabolas, ellipses. Got it?"

"Uh—sure," Rory and I both say. But of course we don't get anything.

"But you're supposed to be dumb. I mean, Thunderdolt Lowenbrow," I say.

"Yep, I know. But guess what?"

"What? "

"I have a secret life," he says, with a trace of smugness.

I'm staring at him really hard. With each passing second, somehow he looks more and more like Eli Weckstein. "Did my mom know? About your secret life?"

"I think so." He smiles. The sparkle in his eyes becomes a glitter. *Nothing wrong in having lots of dreams, sweetie.* Mom's words come back to me now. Eli Thunderdolt Lowenbrow Weckstein certainly fits into her theory of multiple dreams.

"Does your dad know?"

"Of course not." He looks around at his lab. "They don't know what I do here. They think I come up here to moan and groan when I don't want to do 'princely things' like hunt and joust and . . ."

"Marry a princess?" I say.

"Yeah, but as I said, that's not going to happen. By the way, Ryder, call me TD."

"How?" says Rory. "Are you cooking up some potion that can change everyone's minds?"

He regards her with mild contempt. "I told you, I'm not like that quack the Witch of Wenham."

"Then how are we going to do it?" I ask.

"You've taken the first step, Ryder."

"I have?"

"Yes. You crossed over. The next step is a stealth attack. A covert operation, a digital hack, but no one will know about it until the movie premiere."

"You can do this?"

TD nods and says, "I am going to rewrite the computer code for the movie."

I look at all the ancient books on his bookshelves. Books in many different languages, books on science and medicine and astronomy. Ancient! Not one on computer animation.

"I know what you're thinking, Ryder. But I can decode. I've decoded a lot of languages—Hebrew, Aramaic. And if I can decode, I can encode."

"Encode?" Rory and I both say.

"Encode!" His eyes light up. "With a little help, I can write a new script for this movie, and stop what is happening to you."

"But what about what's happening to *you*?"

"I don't mind being thought of as dumb or weird as long as I can have my secret life. I feel a bond with Eli Weckstein. I remember when he was an intern at Starlight. I learned a lot from him by lurking around the portal while he was there." He pauses a long time and looks at me so hard I get goose bumps. "And as for you, Ryder, you are courageous."

Then he swings around to face Rory. "And you too, Rory. You crossed back and forth. For all my smarts, for all the books"—he gestures at his shelves—"I couldn't figure out how to cross over. But you two did. And if you could bring Eli over, that's the help that we need."

"E-Eli? Here?" I stammer. "I'm not sure."

"Eli is brilliant in a twenty-first-century way. My world is post-medieval, pre-Renaissance. A far cry from the digital age. I'm learning as much as I can, as fast as I can, but we need Eli here. Even though I can't cross over, I can listen in on what the animators are doing."

"Do you think Eli could get you up to speed digitally on this?" I say.

"Definitely," TD replies. "And he has a lot of the codes from when he was an intern at Starlight Studios." Prince TD stretches his arms up high and gives a bit of a shake. "Ahhh, this feels so good!"

"What?" I ask.

"Being off script. It's like I get to stretch muscles I've never used before. I'm always off script in the Glower Tower."

"It does feel good," Rory says.

"We have to go off script to change the script," he says.

"Could we add a new character?" I ask.

Rory and TD look a bit befuddled. "Sure, if it'll help," TD says. "What do you have in mind?"

"I've got to think a bit. I might have an idea. But how do you plan to do this, even with Eli's help?"

"I'll definitely need all of your help. We're going to have to go together into the Starlight Studios network . . ." His voice trails off. I get a kind of sickish feeling that maybe he is making this up as he goes along. But what hope do we have? TD takes a step closer to me. "Ryder, do you remember where you were exactly two years ago?"

"No . . . but I know I was happier. It was before Mom died."

"I remember," TD says very solemnly.

"You do?"

"Yes. I'd been hanging around the portal."

"The portal?" I say. TD looks at Rory. She casts her eyes down.

"Rory knows, it's how she got out. I didn't think it would work. But it does. In the real world it's called an Ethernet port. It has to do with connectors between computers and it allows them to communicate with each other."

"No, TD, I do not recall where I was two years ago. So . . . what was I doing?"

"Ryder, it was Take Your Kid to Work Day and your mom and Cassie were going over the storyboards for the movie. And Eli was there too."

"Oh my gosh, I do remember." My voice breaks. I feel

a sob swelling in my throat. "But I—we"—I glance at Rory—"looked fine in those sketches." Rory reaches out with her hand and pats my shoulder very gently. Her touch is as soft as a butterfly, light and deeply tender. Tears glisten in her eyes. Tears glisten in my eyes. We are both seeing our mom's lovely face through a scrim of tears. I've never felt so close to anyone in my life as I do to Rory this minute. It's as if our souls are touching. How can this be?

"You were yourselves. And then everything changed," TD says.

"It sure did," Rory says dully.

"That's the bad news," TD continues. "But the good news is that we can change it back."

"You mean we can rewrite the code?"

TD nods solemnly. "If you can get Eli to cross over."

I take a deep breath. "So, TD, just how do you imagine rewriting the screenplay for *Glo-Rory-Us*?"

"Tomorrow in the real world is Take Your Kid to Work Day. You've got to go with your dad and bring Eli too. You've got to get the passwords and . . . well, I'll give you a list of stuff. Can you do it, Ryder?" He puts his hands on my shoulders and looks me straight in the eye. In that moment he looks so much like Eli Weckstein. It's sort of unbelievable that I didn't notice before.

"Yes, I can do it, but one thing."

"What's that?"

"Time must be different here. How long have I been gone from the real world? It seems like a long time."

"About two minutes."

"That's all?"

"If that," TD says.

"How can that be?"

"Film time. Twenty-four frames per second. So one minute is 1,440 frames. Two is 2,880. Much more happens in one second than in the real world."

"Oh. Even if we're off script?"

"Probably faster," TD says, and Rory nods.

TD presses a piece of paper into my hand. "Take this, Ryder. You'll know what to do."

CHAPTER 15

Back to Reality

Back in my own room, I can hear the party still going on downstairs. The Rory show has ended and the news is on. Did I really go to Ecalpon? I look down at the piece of paper in my hand from TD. It says:

Get password to Cassie's computer. Look for the following of the new movie:

1. Storyboards.

I know what storyboards are: a series of panels that show the overall plan for the story of the movie.

2. Layouts.

Layouts are more detailed panels that show the design, the locations, and the costumes of the characters. I'd seen my parents working on both storyboards and layouts ever since I can remember.

3. Model sheets.

Model sheets show all the possible expressions and postures for a character.

4. Animatics.

The animatics map out the motion and time of each sequence. . . .

5. Texture.

Until the texture stage, the characters and landscapes have been more or less naked. Birds don't have feathers. People don't have skin, and trees are leafless. No clouds in the sky. This is where the digital texture artists came in. Eli knows a lot about texturing because he likes inventing video games. He's creating one right now called *Coming of Rage*. It's about the miracle of the Red Sea. At first the younger characters were way too wild. The game was unplayable. I called the first version *Bar Mitzvah Brats*.

Eli's Rabbi told him the game needs to be an exercise in cooperation and interdependence. No one wins unless the group wins. So Eli went back to work.

It's going to be good.

I look at my list, thinking. All the codes for the Rory show are stored in Cassie's computer as well as those of the other animators. But Cassie's computer has to be the main portal because that computer had been my mom's. It has the original sketches and the very first glimmerings of *Super-Rory-Us*. If we can get to the code in Cassie's computer, we'll have the keys to the kingdom.

The list is five simple words. But there is nothing simple about this. Still, I'll do it for me, Rory, and TD.

I look at the television set. It seems so normal. Had I really gone inside it? Somehow I passed through the portal TD talked about, that interface between the real and the virtual world that allowed Rory and me to trespass the ordinary borders.

I begin thinking about all the books I've ever read where characters in stories go into magical realms. There is of course *Alice in Wonderland*, where Alice sort of dissolves through the looking glass, a mirror, above the mantelpiece. I get the book from my shelf and find the description. There's a picture of her climbing onto the mantel and looking at the mirror. She's talking to her cat. "Let's pretend," she says to the kitty. And in the next minute she describes how the glass got all soft like gauze, so they could get through. Then Alice exclaims, "It's turning into a sort of mist now, I declare!" Within seconds it melts away and bingo—she's through it, dealing with the Red Queen.

I go over to my new television. I put my hand against the glass. "I declare," I mutter. "Shazam?" Nothing happens except a sweaty handprint on the screen. *How did I do it before?* I take a step back and think. If this is really a portal, shouldn't it begin to get bigger or something? Or maybe it should be like the wardrobe in *The Lion, the Witch and the Wardrobe* that Lucy passes through to Narnia, in the part where she exclaims, "This must be an enormous wardrobe," and before she knows it, Shazam! She's standing knee-deep in snow with evergreen branches brushing her face. My TV still looks like a television.

Then I think about what TD said about the Ethernet port. I go over to my computer. The port is a small plug about a half an inch wide. It's hard to imagine squishing into that.

Although Rory was vague about how she got out of Cassie's computer and into my television, it must have been through this portal thing.

I walk over to a table where I have a drawing board set up. I haven't drawn anything since Mom died. But I clear a space on my drawing board and start sketching, feeling my hand unlock for the first time in two years. Two dark eyes loom out at me from the paper. I make them blacker. The eyes of a barn owl. I can't forget that moment in Ecalpon when the owl perched on my shoulder and we looked into each other's eyes as if we understood each other perfectly. No words were needed. Perhaps that was best, because we were completely off script. And I didn't want anyone to hear, because I felt as if someone was watching. And it wasn't Rory. And in that moment as I was drawing I heard a spine-tingling echo.

My name is Contentment but I secretly think of myself as Constance.

This owl, so off script, needs to be in the script. I have to tuck her in someplace. Maybe it's like Mom's quilt—she could always find a spot for something interesting—bit of lace, an old copper coin, a feather! I feel a tingle in my hand. It wants to draw. I want to draw! This owl needs to be drawn. My mom's work is not done.

I sketch sweeping lines. The wings spread as if the owl is about to loft herself into the air. I make tiny strokes on the edges of her heart-shaped face with a soft lead pencil. I give the crown of her head more volume as I shade in some of the darker feathers with another pencil. I am drawing again! I feel a flood of happiness. I feel as if I'm almost flying!

There's a knock on my door.

"Who is it?" I growl.

"Me, Eli."

I open the door and blink, seeing traces of Prince Thunderdolt Lowenbrow in Eli. Not that he looks like a Neanderthal with a projecting forehead. No, it's the sparkle in the eyes. That sparkle makes them kindred spirits. TD said, "I have a secret life." *Like Connie!* I realize. There are many secret lives swirling around me. My head is still filled with the barn owl. She barely had a walk-on part in one episode. She popped out of the rock and then the last image was the back of her wings spread as she flew off. When I saw her in Ecalpon, she was "off script." Her story had just begun and now it needs to be completed.

"You look a little weird," Eli says.

"So do you. . . . Oh, I mean you look fine."

"You're acting a little weird." He tips his head to one side and studies me. "But maybe I would too if that woman and her daughters were hanging around."

"Yeah, pretty gross."

"Is that why you bugged out of the party?"

"Uh, sort of."

"Can I come in? The party is really boring."

"Sure," I say, and scoot over and turn off the TV. I don't want any surprises. It's a little odd being back in the real world. Especially since I'm trying to figure out how to tell him that his talents are needed in a make-believe place. When I asked TD if Mom knew of his secret life, he nodded and his eyes burned brighter and he said, "I think so." But does Eli know? Should I ask him? Should I tell him? Is he meant to know? It's way over my head. But then again, I'm supposed to recruit Eli. So maybe I should tell him.

"How's the video game going?"

"Pretty good. My rabbi likes it."

"He does? Wow!"

"Yeah, you see, all these people are shoving to get across the Red Sea in time, but I built in this move where if you help an old person, you get across quicker. So it's like . . . lessons in cooperation, supporting others, that kind of stuff."

Cooperation, I think, *supporting others.* Rory, TD, and I could be part of his bar mitzvah project.

"Oh, that reminds me." I try to be casual. "Tomorrow is Take Your Kid to Work Day. Are you going with your dad?"

"No! That would be totally boring."

"Your mom? You could go with her."

"My mom? Are you crazy? She's an obstetrician. I don't want to see a baby being born and I doubt the mothers want me there either."

"Eek! Yeah! I forgot."

"So are you going back to the party?" Eli asks.

"Nah. I'm pretending to be sick. Well, I did throw up."

"I don't blame you." He looks down at his feet. "I

mean, this must be really, really hard for you, Ryder—
Bernice and all. Those daughters."

Eli suddenly looks as if he is about to cry. "I miss your
mom too, Ryder."

I want to tell Eli everything that happened to me and
how TD wants me to bring him across. But I can't seem
to find the words. How do you explain something like
this? *Hey, Eli, I got news for you. The virtual world is not
exactly virtual. In some ways it's more real than the real
world.* I mean, isn't this like saying a thousand years
ago or so, *Listen up, everybody. The world is not flat. It's
round!* "Uh, Eli . . ."

"What?"

"Nothing, I guess."

"Then I'll go find my parents. Maybe they're ready to
go. So . . ."

"Okay, see you around. Good luck on your game."

"Thanks."

Eli gives a little wave, and it's almost princely. No finger waggles, just a slow turn of his palm as if to take in
the multitudes when riding by in a coach.

I go back to my notebook and make little sketches,
just the way Mom used to when she worked out the design for a character. I do close-ups of the barn owl's face.
I concentrate on getting the light just right in her eyes.
There has to be a little glint, a reflection or two. I remember Mom working hard on characters' eyes. "Eyes

are the window to the soul," Mom would say. I think she was quoting some ancient writer. I want to find the soul that stirs in this owl. And what is soul? A kind of spiritual wireframe? Perhaps a secret life—something unchanging, constant and forever.

CHAPTER 16

. . . .

A Sob in the Night

I finish the last of my drawings around one in the morning. I should have told Eli last night about crossing over and meeting Rory, but I had no idea that I'd get so far with my drawings of Constance the owl. She's vital in some way to saving Rory, saving the movie. I know it. I need Eli to bring Constance to life, in wireframe, and then textured—feathers and all. I spent a good two hours online studying barn owl feathers. Very soft, subtle colors, speckled with white spots.

I text him.

Need help. Need to wireframe and texture. Things are changing in Ecalpon.

I get excited when I hear a bing! It's not Eli, but Penny—Penelope.

You'll never guess! I met a prince. Prince Ludlow of Luxembourg. Isn't that title fab????

I don't text her back, but I think, *I met a prince too. A virtual one, and he's also pretty fab.*

A few minutes pass and no answer from Eli. I wander to the kitchen. There must be some good leftovers from the party. I cram three cocktail weenies into my mouth at once—and right then I hear someone crying in the home theater. I look in and see that it's Connie, heaped on the floor in a corner. Her entire body is shaking.

"Connie?" No answer. "Connie." I tap her shoulder. She raises her head. "Are you all right?"

"You'd never understand!" She seems almost angry.

"Why are you here? Why didn't you go home after the party with your mom and sisters?"

"Because I hate them and they hate me. The only person who ever loved me was my dad."

"Oh no! Did he get hurt on his science trip?"

"Worse."

"What do you mean?"

"My email to him bounced back. Then I sent a letter to his last known address. It came back. 'Return to Sender, Addressee Unknown.'"

"I'm sorry, Connie. You must be so upset. Your sisters too."

"He's not their father."

"Oh," I say.

"Bliss and Joy are from my mom's first and second marriages."

"She's been married three times?"

Connie nods.

"But I still don't understand. Why did you stay here for the night?"

"We had a big fight. They always side with her."

"What was the fight about?"

"They say I'm a drag. That I spoil everything, all because I was trying to find Dad. They just gang up on me sometimes. So I said I wouldn't go home with them after the party. Your dad said I could stay here."

"In the home theater."

"No. I thought I'd watch some TV. I actually watched your show. *Super-Rory-Us*. It's sort of fun."

"You liked it?"

"Yeah, I saw the one where the witch tries to turn the owl into a rock so she can get gold." She gives a sly little smile, then adds, "Sound familiar?"

I blink. Is she saying what I think she might be saying? Is she that smart? Or is she saying that her mom is a gold digger?

"Oh, Constance!" I whisper.

"Constance?" Her face breaks into a huge smile. "You're calling me Constance?"

"Sure."

"Is the owl in any other episodes? My dad really likes owls."

"My mom liked them too. I think she would have had the character continue, but . . ." I look down at my hands.

Constance doesn't say anything for a minute. "You know, my dad is a member of the Audubon Society."

"Really?" Somehow I cannot imagine Bernice being married to a member of the Audubon Society.

"Yep. He's a birder. A real lister."

"Lister?"

"Yeah, he identifies birds in the wild. I used to go with him."

"Where?"

"Virginia. But someday we were planning on going someplace really exotic, like Patagonia, in South America."

"Owling?"

"Yeah! You go out at night and you listen. And when you hear one, it's haunting. Magical. And you know what the most beautiful owl sound is?"

"Don't they all just hoot?"

"Oh, no, not at all. The most beautiful sound is the one made by screech owls."

"Really?"

"Yep. Really. They don't screech at all. It's like chimes." Constance closes her eyes. I can tell she's remembering being with her dad, listening to the magical sound of an owl.

At that moment my phone bings. "Got to take this." I run back to my bedroom. It's from Eli. *Call me now.*

"Eli, this is really hard to explain on the phone. But you've got to come to Starlight Studios with me tomorrow. Things are happening that you won't believe."

"Like what?"

"I've crossed over."

"Crossed over to where?"

"Ecalpon."

"Huh?"

"I know, it's crazy! But I need your help. We all need your help."

"Who's we?"

"Me, Rory, Prince Thunderdolt Lowenbrow."

"Ryder, you're talking as if they're real. This is hard to understand—it's the middle of the night!"

"I know, sorry! But they're real. You need to come with me, first to Starlight Studios, then to Ecalpon."

"I have a parkour practice. It's free running—my specialty."

"Okay. When can you get to the studio?"

"By lunch at the latest."

"Okay . . . and . . ."

"Yes?"

"Prepare yourself."

"For what?"

"Going to Ecalpon!"

CHAPTER 17

●●●●●●●●●●●●●●●●●●

The Teardrop

It's midmorning the day after the party, and I'm at Starlight Studios with my owl drawings. I don't want anyone in the studio to see them. I used to think the place where they "Make Magic Happen" was the coolest. Not anymore.

I like my sketches, but to make Constance into a fully animated character takes a lot of code, a lot of programming. Since the owl was on-screen only briefly in that one episode, not much code exists for her. Eli cannot get here soon enough.

"Ryder." Cassie looks up at me from a layout for a new show about dinosaurs. "I have to go to a meeting, so I hope you don't mind being here on your own. It should only be about a half hour. You can go back to the texture files I showed you earlier and fiddle around with the T. rex skin."

You bet I'm going to fiddle around, I think. *But not with any dinosaur skin.* Feathers. My barn owl needs plumage. "Oh, cool!" I say. I'm becoming a terrific pretender, or maybe a liar. Strange, I pretend more in the real world than in the make-believe world.

Earlier, Cassie showed me how they made the textures for the dinosaurs' skins. The digital programming has certainly advanced since I sat on Mom's lap as a five-year-old. But Eli must know all about this.

"I can pick up some lunch for us," Cassie says. "What would you like?"

"Pizza!" I say quickly. "And remember, Eli is coming."

"I left a pass for him at the desk. You know, the commissary is pretty slow with the pizza."

I almost blurt out, *I know, that's why I want it!* Instead I say, "That's fine, I'm not hungry yet." I need to buy all the time I can. TD said time is slower in Ecalpon, but I'm nervous. What if our plan doesn't work? And I keep wondering if I should've told Constance what I have planned for Constance the owl in Ecalpon. No—I need to get the barn owl fully rendered. Dad seemed pleased when he came into the kitchen this morning and found me and Constance talking. He invited her to stay for a few days until things "blow over." So she's going to be around.

Cassie stops at the door and composes her face into an imitation of jolliness. "Have a good time with that texturing program."

"Oh, that'll be fun." *Lies, lies, lies,* I think. I'm doomed to die in a cesspool of lies. But Starlight Studios is murdering my virtual self and it feels as if the dagger is plunging directly into my very real heart. That heart is thudding away at the moment so loudly I'm afraid Cassie will hear it.

"I'll set it up for you before I go." She comes back to the computer. This could be a real break! I might not have to wait for Eli to come with the codes.

My eyes are glued to the keyboard as she types. *Ryder, if you ever used your brain, use it now. Remember that password.* Cassie's fingers move fast but I get it.

Cassie gets up to leave. "See you soon, Ryder. Pizza, any special toppings?"

"No," I say quickly. I don't want thoughts of pepperoni when I'm trying to remember her password. I scribble it on scrap paper, get my drawings, and go to scan them in. Then it's back to the computer keyboard.

Password works, I'm in! But, what's happening? I'm transported into a weird ghostly landscape swirling with fog. "This is just too strange," I mutter.

"No! This is perfect." Dim voices are coming toward me and spectral figures advance.

"Welcome to the land of wireframes." It's TD. He's lumbering toward me. Rory is by his side. They look like mummies but walk like zombies.

"Wireframes?" I whisper. They are sort of like mannequins, solid but at the same time blank, no faces, no skin.

"That's not you, Rory! It can't be." I am looking at a shape that is *waaaayyyy* too old for me or for Rory. And I don't mean Granny-type old. And something else is different too: from the top of her head, gleaming hair falls down straight past her shoulders. Not a curl or a cowlick in sight.

"It can't be you," I whisper.

Then this blank face begins to speak. "It won't be me!" There is a chilling disconnect between the voice and the body as Rory stomps her foot just the way I do when I am mad. But things jiggle where they shouldn't. She's moving toward me but not exactly walking. More like tottering. There is something awfully familiar about it. It can't be. I stare at the figure's feet. Rory is right. This *is* Bliss.

"Those boots?"

The figure that is supposed to be Rory sighs. "Stiletto heels. I suppose you could say they're a kind of weapon."

"What happened to your slingshot, your bow and arrow?"

"Gone! Gone! Gone!"

Rory of course told me all this, but now it's right in front of me.

And then something very strange happens. A tiny oval begins to sparkle just beneath where her eye should be on the wireframe. I step closer.

"Rory, are you crying?"

"I think so, but I'm in wireframe. I'm off script. I'm not even in Ecalpon yet, right?"

TD's eyeless face seems to peer at her. "This has to be a miracle of some sort. I . . . I . . . I don't believe in miracles. . . . I believe in science . . . the science of animation."

"What do you mean, you don't believe in miracles?" I say. "All this is a miracle—Rory stepping out of my television set, me going into your world—it's all miraculous." I think of Eli's game. "And what about the Red Sea closing for Moses?"

"Moses? Red Sea? What does that have to do with me?" TD asks. "Am I Jewish?"

"What do you think? My mom based you on Eli."

"I'm a Jewish prince!" he exclaims. I nod. He says, "Moses? I'm Moses?"

"Not quite, buster!"

"But you just said that your mom invented me and

I told you I felt that she knew about my . . . er . . . uh . . ."

"Secret life?" Then I remember Constance and the owl sketches. But I don't think this is the time to bring up my idea for a new character.

"Yes, my interest in science, and you said I reminded you of that boy Eli that your mom used as a model for me. And you were going to bring him across. Where is he?"

"I'm hoping he will be here soon."

"Eli Weckstein! Could he teach me parkour? It's so much more interesting than jousting. Don't you think?"

"I guess."

But TD's suddenly very quiet, watching the wireframe of Rory. Another tear melts out of her featureless face. He lifts a finger and touches her cheek.

"It is a miracle," he whispers quietly as Rory stifles a sob. "She's crying real tears. I feel it." He touches her cheek again. Until this moment TD and Rory were animated characters in a make-believe world, and right now they are both just skeletons of those characters caught in the in-between space of wireframe. However, those faceless wireframes of TD and Rory are looking at me as if they have eyes.

TD suddenly bursts out, "Ryder, you don't understand how much of a miracle this is. We have no skin, no faces, no color. This cannot be happening. There

cannot be tears, not yet. That is the miracle. The miracle of Rory!"

There is a soft whirring noise, then a sort of bleep, and a very metallic sound as if a trash can has been turned over. A real one, not a virtual one.

"Eli!" I shout.

"Yeah. Where am I?" He staggers toward me. "Holy moly, WIREFRAME!" he exclaims. "But I don't understand. The codes worked. But this is—"

"I know, Eli. This is just a way station on the road to Ecalpon."

TD now comes up. "Allow me to introduce myself. No need to bow. I am a scientist first. A prince second. It's very low on my list of priorities. We have just experienced a miracle."

"*You've* experienced a miracle!" Eli says. "What about me? What have I experienced?"

Then there's a fluttering in the air.

"What's that?" everyone says at once.

"My sketches for a new character who I think can help us. We're writing her back into the script. This is our choice, our chance to make things right. But she's not in wireframe yet," I reply.

"I know where the codes are," Eli says.

"How can she help us?" Rory asks.

"In 'real life' she's Connie."

"Connie?" Rory gasps. "One of the Three Happys?"

"Yes."

"But Ryder, they're the enemy."

"Not Connie. I mean Constance. She is like her name. Steadfast and true."

"An enemy you can trust? Ryder, you better be right or we'll be in big trouble."

RORY

CHAPTER 18

The Miracle That Is Me

I could tell Ryder was very confused when that tear slipped from my nonexistent eyes. From Ryder's point of view, my wireframe crying might not be a big deal. She might think it was a glitch in the code. But I believe this tear is the kind of miracle that comes straight out of a fairy tale, like in "Sleeping Beauty" when the prince wakes her up with a kiss. Sort of. Thank heaven I didn't have to kiss TD and he didn't have to kiss me. The tear has nothing to do with any prince. It is simply magical.

I turn and begin to lumber toward Ryder. She shrinks back a bit. I do look sort of like a zombie.

"Ryder, listen to me. If this can happen"—I point to my cheek—"if this tear is real . . ."

"It looks very real, Rory. More real than the rest of you."

I know she's looking at my body and I feel her eyes traveling down to the stiletto-heeled boots. Of course, that's just the front of me. I turn slightly. "And you're not going to believe my butt. Look at it!"

"I'd rather not," Ryder says.

"This is terrible." Eli is stunned. "My dad had hinted that there were some changes Cassie wasn't pleased with."

"That's an understatement. But Eli, if this is real, this tear, it means things can change. We can change them. The four of us," I say.

"Maybe the five of us," Ryder says.

"Oh—the owl," Eli says.

"Rory is right." TD has fire in his voice. "We can change all of it."

"Where do we begin?" Ryder asks.

"With me," I cry. "Get rid of the high-heeled boots. I want my old ones back. I can't walk, run, or ride a horse in these things. And most important, I want my old body back."

"You do kind of defy gravity," Ryder says.

"No," TD replies. "You've got it wrong. If she defied the laws of gravity, she would be floating."

"And this stupid wand." I toss it as hard as I can.

"*Hasta la vista!*" Ryder yells, getting into the spirit.

"Here's what we've got to do," TD says. "Sneak our old selves, our true selves, back into these wireframes."

Eli is nearly jumping out of his skin—he's so lucky to have skin to jump out of. It's not exactly skin as he knew it. He's arrived as a cartoon just as Ryder did when she came to Ecalpon.

"I think I know what you're talking about, TD—a Trojan horse," Eli says.

"What's that?" I ask.

"It's from history," Ryder answers.

TD steps closer. "There was this ancient city of Troy, and the Greeks wanted to get inside and capture it. They created this huge wooden horse and all of the best Greek soldiers climbed into it. The Trojans thought they had captured a war trophy and pulled the horse inside the city gates, but guess what?"

"The soldiers jumped out of the horse and took the city!" I gasp.

"Shazam!" Ryder exclaims. "And Eli can write a Trojan horse program to undo what has been done to you, Rory. Get your body and boots back. Bury all the good stuff deep in the wireframe so they can't find it. Then it will pop out for the movie premiere. Can't you, Eli?"

"Absolutely."

"I get it now," I say. "We're kind of like the secret soldiers."

• • •

"But how?" I ask. "You make it seem so easy."

"We're in the best starting place we can be," Eli says. "Right here in wireframe with you. I just have to find the trash."

"I think you stumbled over it when you came in, Eli," Ryder says.

"The trash?" TD and I say. "There's no real trash in our land," I say. "We have slop pails in the barn, but they're just props."

"Yes, it's virtual trash here," Ryder says. She seems very cheerful for some reason. "But please remember we're not all the way into make-believe." She goes on. "We're in the outskirts. That's what wireframe is. On every computer screen there's a little trash can icon. So what we got to do is . . ."

"Empty it?" I say.

"NOOOOOO!" Ryder is jumping up and down in complete alarm. "Never empty it. Carefully unpack what we need. It's full of valuable things that you need to get your old self back. Your old body, your old boots, your bow and arrow. And then we'll save them in a hidden place until just the right moment, when they spring to life. Or, pardon me, into a full-blown animation." Ryder steps up very close. "Rory, you're right." Her voice is grave. "Your tear is real and miraculous.

This is the magic that will let our plan happen like a true fairy tale—our electronic Tinker Bell moment, our Sleeping Beauty moment—just watch. A tear and a trash can. That's all we need."

At that I shed another tear. This time a tear of true happiness.

RYDER

CHAPTER 19

A Tear and a Trash Can

Aladdin's cave could not have spilled over with as many riches as that virtual trash can on Cassie's computer. We unpacked it as if we were handling precious gems. The first thing we found was the ax I always dreamed of for Rory.

It's an ax or maybe a sword—a *swax*! The curve of the blade and the handle are works of art. In a bottom corner of the scanned drawing are Cassie's initials, CGS. "Can you see this, guys?" I ask. "I mean, since you don't have eyes yet."

"I can see it!" Rory says breathlessly. "I think it's my tears. They're like a lens."

"I can almost see it," TD says. He bends very close

to the sketch. I see Rory raising her wireframe hand as if she is imagining how she might grasp this weapon. "Goldarn, what I could do with this blade."

"Rory, you sound like Granny." We grin at each other.

"Well, she is sort of my granny too, Ryder."

"But you've never met her."

"I know, but she kind of seeped into me somehow."

"Digital genetics?" Eli mutters. "Let's see what else is in the trash can!"

We find sketches and texture codes for Rory's old hairstyle. There is code for everything: body types, faces, animals. Eli and I sort all of this out.

"Okay," I finally say. "I think we have the 'guts' for our Trojan horse. Now we need another trash can to put this in for when we want it."

"Maybe a locked trash can," TD says. "One that only we know the combination to."

"Good idea," Eli says.

"But where can we hide it?" I ask.

"In plain sight?" TD says.

"What do you mean?" Rory asks.

"Put it inside the other trash can," TD says.

"In the trash icon on Cassie's desktop screen?" I ask.

"Exactly! A trash can within a trash can."

"Brilliant!" Eli shouts. I see a little kindling flicker between Eli and the wireframe of TD where his eyes might be. Eli knows that he is the secret version of Prince Thunderdolt Lowenbrow.

The secret trash can becomes our Trojan horse. We pick a secure password. But I'm still worried. It seems risky.

A shadow flickers by. "What's that?" Rory asks as a scan of one of the sketches of the owl lands on her shoulder.

"Constance! I nearly forgot. Eli, can you take these scans and figure out how to wireframe her?"

"Sure, we have a few of the original codes your mom worked on."

"I'm still not sure how she'll help us." Rory lifts a wireframe hand to her shoulder to pet the shadowy owl.

"Here's the code," Eli says. He works silently, studying my scans as he rewires the shapes.

"What are you doing?" TD asks. "Remember, our eyes are mostly off duty."

"Oh, yes. Sorry. Wireframing is taking something flat, like Ryder's sketches, and turning it into a 3-D object. Sort of like a 3-D jigsaw puzzle. When I complete the rewire, the image of Constance the owl will appear to have volume."

I can't stay much longer. I need to get back to Cassie's office. As I turn to leave, I trip over a file called Product Projections.

"Just one second," I say. There are some numbers: 36—22—41. Hmmm. Is this a code or a password? No. I see a chart with "Doll Figure Analogs" written at the top. It shows a picture of Bliss in a skintight dress and then a miniature Bliss in a princess outfit. It's the brand-new Princess Rory doll! It all comes back to me—the Sugar Babe store and the banner announcing a *Bling Blast* that would help release your inner princess. Well, this inner princess was going right back inside, never to come back, I hope.

Suddenly there's a crackling sound. I feel a current pass through me. My cowlicks stand up and then everything goes black. I'm dead!

Okay. Not quite dead. I smell pizza, and I'm sitting in Cassie's desk chair as she comes in.

"Eli, when did you pop in?"

He looks at the clock and blinks. "Oh, a little while ago," he says. He must have thought we were gone for hours.

Cassie sets down the pizza. "Power outage," she mutters. A little bell rings. "That's the computer switching over to the battery and restarting."

"How was your meeting?" I ask.

"Oh, fine," Cassie says. She looks down and concentrates on the pizza as she opens the lid. "Your dad hasn't talked to you about the movie or anything yet?" she asks nervously.

"Nah, you know he's busy."

Dad walks in.

"How you doin', sweetheart? Ah, Eli! Glad you could come over. You two having fun with Cassie? Whatcha been up to?"

"Oh, nothing, really," I lie. I'm back in the real world. So of course I lie here.

"Before I left for the meeting, I was showing Ryder the texturing we're doing on the dinosaurs," Cassie says.

"Grrrreatt!" Dad says a little too enthusiastically. I look at him. *Unhinged,* I think, *just slightly unhinged.* "Unhinged" was a favorite word of Mom's, but as far as I know she never used it about Dad.

The overhead lights come on and I glance at the computer. It's back on regular power. The screen looks the way it did when Cassie left, not a trace of the wireframes or of my sketches of the owl Constance. But my eyes linger on the trash can. I hope and pray it's all still there.

Cassie's showing Dad the texture for the T. rex that I had helped her work on.

Dad pats me on the back. "You'll be an old pro in no time! Just like your mom!" I wince, but as I watch the screen I sense something behind the stippling texture of the dinosaur skin program. It's them! Rory and TD and Constance! Looking out at me! Listening just the way Rory said they could when they spy on the animators.

I can almost hear their whispers. The owl hoots softly as if to say, "If only . . ." *If only what?* I wonder. Then a thrilling quickness stirs inside me. "Hey, Dad, I was just thinking, since Constance—"

"Who?"

"Connie. Since she's staying at our house now, she could come to Starlight with me sometime."

"What a nice idea. Glad you and Connie are getting along."

Dad's face breaks into a huge smile. I look at him and sigh inside.

If not for Bernice, Rory would have never been changed, been made over into the image of Bliss. What spells has Bernice cast on Dad? What an absolute witch she is! But soon Constance will meet up with her secret self. And when she does, she might be able to help us. She'll know what to do.

PART
II

CHAPTER 20

Her Name Is Constance

I am holding my breath as Constance sifts through my sketches of the owl on the floor in my bedroom.

"Ryder, these are beautiful. You're a true artist, just like your mom."

"You think so?"

"Yes." She looks at me with those luminous black eyes. I really did get the flickers of light just right in them.

"Does the owl remind you of anyone?"

Constance shakes her head. "The owl is . . . a she?"

"Yeah."

"What's her name?" She looks at me expectantly. "You haven't named her yet?"

"Oh, I've named her."

"Can you tell me? Or is it a secret?"

"It's your secret, Constance."

She rocks back on her knees. "What do you mean?"

"I mean I named her for you. Her name is Constance."

"But . . . why me?"

"Because she is you. She is steadfast and loyal and searching, but most of all she is constant to herself."

"You really think that about me?"

"I do. But there's more. . . . This is going to be very hard for me to explain."

"Try, Ryder." She reaches out and her hand touches mine. It's as if a feather brushed across it.

"You know there have been changes made to Rory. She's older and more like—"

"Bliss," she says dully. "You aren't supposed to know. How did you find out?"

"Rory."

"Rory? How could she tell you? What did she do, pop out of the television screen and say, 'Hey, they're changing me'?"

"Yes, that's exactly what she did," I say, matter-of-fact.

She gasps. "You're not kidding, are you?"

I reach for the remote. The television is connected to the Ethernet port on my computer. Eli devised this. The quickest way to Ecalpon. I turn to Constance. "I'm not kidding." Reaching out, I take her hand. "Constance, come with me to Ecalpon."

As I click the remote her hand turns into a wing and we are off.

THE WITCH OF WENHAM

CHAPTER 21

Super Byogen!

From the high window of the tower of the Lizard Stone, the Witch of Wenham peers through her spyglass. She mutters as she catches sight of four children. Yet another miserable kid from the real world has come across.

"Those brats! These scrapulous, clapper-clawed miscreants. Beslubbering little toads. Fie! Fie on them, the little sun-ripened pig droppings!" There are not enough words in the Witch of Wenham's treasury of curses, oaths, and slander for her to fling at the children now scampering around the hills and dales of Ecalpon.

"And that's my owl!"

"Your owl, madam?" Jeeves the lizard looks out the narrow window from the shoulders of his mistress.

"Yes, my very own. The one I turned into a rock and that vile child Rory turned back into an owl again. Next she was written out of the script and I never had another crack at my alchemy. I came the closest with her, you know."

"Whatever you see happening now with that owl will be off script, madam. There are no plans to bring her back into the series or the movie."

"Hrrrumph!" the witch growls, and squints. "Look, she's got another kid with her."

"Ah, yes, Eli of Weck from the real world."

"Real world!" the witch growls. *It was bad enough,* the witch thinks, *when it was just Rory and that fool girl Ryder who had somehow slipped through from* that *world into hers!* "I'll show them what's real!"

"Madam," Jeeves says, "we cannot toy with what is real. We are make-believe!"

"That means nothing. And furthermore, you are *not* supposed to disagree with me, you . . . you revolting little thing. You're my servant . . . my . . . my . . ."

"Butler, madam. I'm a butler. I was named for a very famous butler in English literature."

"Well, start acting like a butler. Fetch me some tea."

"Yes, madam." The lizard scrambles down from the witch's arms to the stone floor. With a little bow, asks, "One lump or two?"

"Fourteen, you numskull, you know how I love sugar."

"Yes, of course." Then he whispers to himself, "That's why you only have one tooth left."

Jeeves the lizard brings the tea. The witch is perched again by the window, watching the children work on their secret project. Well, not so secret to those in Ecalpon, but definitely secret to Starlight Studios. *They are clever little devils,* thinks the witch. *Eli of Weck is uncommonly bright. Put him together with Prince Thunderdolt and it is a dangerous combination. Who would have thought that dull prince was so smart?* The witch has always thought he went up into his tower to sulk. Not so. Jeeves, her spy, had reported alarming developments. The most staggering were the changes they had made to the creation of her own long-lost daughter, Byogen, the inspiration for the new Rory.

If her daughter rose to royalty, the witch would have a much bigger part in the series and the future movies. All this had become possible when Ralph met that new woman she had heard Rory talking about. Bernice is her ticket to success. Fate has planned this. The show could be retitled *Super Byogen.* Though *Super Bliss* would be fine. She turns to Jeeves, who is perched again on her shoulder.

"I had so many hopes, Jeeves. You know, that woman Bernice is a mother just like me. We both have deeply maternal instincts. She's a woman after my own heart."

"But, madam, we're not real. We don't have hearts or lungs, or livers or spleens or—"

"Creature, shut up. I might not have a heart, but I have something here." She slaps her chest.

Jeeves hates it when his mistress calls him "creature." He wants to say, *You have nothing there. Some of us, especially characters like Rory, have a flickering of some indefinable tenderness deep in our wireframe souls.* But the lizard slinks off.

The witch squints out the window. The clouds clear and she has a good view of the small farm where Rory's family lives. She spies Bethilda.

"God's teeth, that fool is curtsying to the chickens." She runs her fingers fretfully through her thin hair, which hovers over her head like a tangle of electrified spider webs.

Bethilda's practicing! Practicing for the Princess Rory's arrival and coronation! The old biddy wants a princess in this kingdom as much as I do, thinks the witch.

The witch mutters, "She wants to improve her own lot. Just like me! She's my secret weapon. No more feeding chickens. I need to go among the peasants and have a talk with dear Bethilda."

Jeeves shivers.

RYDER

CHAPTER 22

Hearts!

"This is just incredible," Eli murmurs. It's the first time he has made it all the way into Ecalpon, past the wireframe. It's also his first time meeting Rory and TD as fully animated characters. "It's exactly like your mom drew this place, except more. I mean, I can feel the wind."

"Me too!" Constance murmurs as the wind stirs the delicate fringe feathers at the edges of her wings.

"Hey, Ryder," he says, "I thought Constance the owl wasn't able to talk."

"She's off script," Rory and I both answer.

"She can talk all she wants when she's off script," TD adds. "We all do."

"Constance, you don't mind about the nontalking role, do you?" I ask.

"Not at all. And besides, I get to fly. I'd swap talking for flying any day." She spreads her wings and sails into the sky.

I tip my head back and track her flight. It must be beautiful to see Ecalpon from up there—the meadows sprinkled with wild flowers and divided by sparkling creeks; the castle of TD, its towers and turrets poking the clouds. Constance is a beautiful flier.

"It's so wonderful to see her." I sigh. "Eli, you did a fantastic job with the texture. You got the feathers just right—the tawny colors, the white spots melting out of the darker feathers, and the delicate white ones for her heart-shaped face. Just perfect."

We have walked out to the Lizard Stone, where the Witch of Wenham lives up in her tower.

"She's probably watching us. She spies on everybody," Rory says.

I don't care that much about the witch, but I want to see the lizards scamper on the rocky headland that juts into the water. I have a faint memory of Mom first drawing them. She had all these pictures pinned up in her home office of iguanas and monitor lizards, geckos, all kinds of reptiles with feet. Some of their scales were beautiful. "Like tapestries," Mom said. But it was their eyes that fascinated me. They have a vertical slit in each eye that flashes when their pupils contract. Just as I'm thinking about them, one scampers across our path, turns, and looks directly at me as if it wants to talk. The yellowish eyes flash and suddenly there's a familiar electric blue slit. I feel as if it took me in with that one flicker. The lizard scampers off.

We turn and walk off in another direction and Rory takes us down a narrow dusty lane lined with hedgerows.

"What's that?" Eli asks. A sign with an arrow points ahead: EAST GRIEF. Below the top arrow is another sign: THE VALLEY OF DELETIONS.

"It's the dump," Rory says. "Ideas that didn't work— bits of dialogue, scans of very preliminary sketches, failed special effects."

"They didn't just put them in the trash can?" I ask.

"Probably," Eli says. "On the computer, when you finally dump out your trash can, when you open that tab that says 'Empty Trash' and click, this is where it ends up."

"I see," I say. The road to East Grief dips down and we continue walking. A cold fog creeps in.

"This is the foggiest place in Ecalpon." Rory puts her arm through mine.

We are silent; we've been walking down into the valley for quite a while. Fragments of scripts swirl about our feet. Occasionally Constance flies out ahead to bring back a scrap of something. She has very good vision despite the fog.

"Look at this!" Constance says, and drops a very rough sketch of a baby.

"What's this?" Rory asks.

"Whoa!" I say. "Rory, it's us as a baby. Mom thought us up when I was an infant. You know that."

"How did our mom ever get inspired changing stinky diapers all day long?" Rory asks.

"She must have thought ahead, imagined us as middle school kids. I bet these sketches would have been used as a prologue," I say. "Like 'Once upon a time, in a land far, far away, a very adorable baby was born. . . .'" Everyone starts laughing. Constance's owl laugh is like a snuffy hiccup.

"You're calling yourself adorable?" Eli says.

"First of all, it's not just me. I'm calling Rory adorable too. And secondly . . ." I can't think of what's second. I just know that I'm suddenly very sad. "Let's go," I snap. An idea pops into my brain.

Rory turns to me. "Ryder, what is it? You've thought of something."

"I certainly have! Remember the Trojan horse, where we're hiding all the things until we're ready and then unlocking it all to work like a time bomb?"

"Yeah?" Eli says.

" 'Bomb' is the wrong word."

"So?" Eli and Rory both ask.

"We're rebuilding, re-creating what was originally meant to be. I'm worried about the double-trash-can thing."

"You mean the double encryption? It's way better than the double trash cans," Eli says.

"What if we hide the Trojan horse here in the Valley of Deletions!" I say.

Eli's mouth forms a huge O but no sound comes out.

"Brilliant!" Rory shouts.

I rush on. "This is where we can be sure things won't be found. And I'll bet anything there is a direct path from here up to the trash can on the computers of Starlight Studios, for where else would trash go when they click on 'Empty Trash'? Don't you think so, Eli?"

"Ryder, this is an awesome strategy!"

I look at Eli. He's already had the great idea today of hooking up our home computers to the television through the Ethernet port, which gets us instantly to the trash can on Cassie's desktop and then directly into Ecalpon. But now we need an even quicker connection to the Valley of Deletions.

"Eli, could you write some new code that will get us straight to the Valley of Deletions? This is where our work has to be done."

"Of course I can write that code. And we'll call it the Trash Can Trail!" Eli shouts.

"You're a genius!" I clap.

"No, Ryder. It's your idea. It's good! Not just good—brilliant!"

"In real time it's less than one week until the premiere," Rory says.

"I think the Trash Can Trail will speed things up for us," I say.

We find the direct trail from the Valley of Deletions to the trash can icon on the computers of Starlight Studios, and then can easily jump to our own computers. As if to confirm this discovery, someone at Starlight Studios dumps their trash and a blizzard of digital garbage pours down on us. Little black bits and pieces of code are swirling about our heads. Eli swiftly pieces together the bits so that we can use the trash can icons to cross over and to keep our trail hidden.

We wind our way back to Rory's cottage, where we gather round the table for some bread and honey mead broth. Bread and honey mead broth seem to be all they eat in Ecalpon.

"And what about the coronation?" Rory sighs as she takes a sip of the broth. "That will be so gross."

"I don't care about the coronation. That's minor," I say.

"Minor!" TD, Rory, and Eli explode.

"Permit me, Ryder," TD says. "If I may take just a

moment—say 720 frames. I'm a prince. I know about coronations and this is nothing to be casual about. You *do not* want to do one or attend one. They're a great waste of money and time that could be better spent on improving the lot of the villagers, farming techniques, education."

"But it's Bliss who is going to be crowned at Starlight Land. Not me. Not Rory. Let Bliss have her day. I don't care."

"Yes," Constance says, nodding, "let Bliss have her day." She's perched on a rafter, looking down at us. "The coronation happens before the movie premiere by several hours. The shock value of the movie when the original Rory is revealed will be even greater if there's a coronation beforehand."

"You are living up to your reputation for wisdom, owl," Eli says.

"You are so right, Constance." Rory's eyes grow as big as saucers. "I'm not going to worry about a stupid real girl getting a fake crown. It's the movie that counts. In this case the virtual world is going to be much more real and truthful than the real world."

I look at Rory with amazement. "Oh, Rory!" I say in awe. "Our hearts are in the virtual world."

Now tears glisten in Rory's eyes. "You think I really do have a heart, Ryder? Even though I'm just a cartoon?"

"Of course you do. And so do you, TD. You both have

every bit as much of a heart as either Eli or me or Constance. You've got heart." I hug them.

Then, "Let's get started!" Rory says.

We work feverishly. In Ecalpon the sun begins to set. TD has to get back to his castle. Rory's parents have returned from the Coddington market with Bethilda, who shuffles about, downcast.

"So you think maybe you can make things all right again?" Rory's mom asks.

"Yes, we will, Mum," Rory says.

"But what can you do exactly?" Rory's dad asks.

"It has to do with the wireframes, Da. You know, those are sort of our basic skeletons. Before they texture us."

I'm looking at Bethilda, and have a funny feeling. She's listening awfully carefully.

Rory turns to me. "Speaking of texture," she says, "Ryder changed my hair back."

I give Rory a quick kick under the table and flick my eyes toward Bethilda.

Rory gets it immediately and changes the subject. "I mean, don't worry, Mum. I think things will be fine."

I say it's time to leave, time for us to go back to the real world via the trash can icon on Cassie's computer. Eli walks ahead while Constance lights on my shoulder.

"We're still off script, right? So I can talk."

"Of course. What's up?"

"You're kind of jittery."

"I'm worried someone could follow us to the Valley of Deletions and find out about our 'laboratory,' as Eli calls it, and Cassie is no fool. My dad? Well, he wasn't a fool until he met your mom. Sorry."

"Don't feel sorry. I agree."

"Was your dad a fool too, Constance?" I ask.

"I think so. A sweet fool, like your dad."

"Why won't he call you or write you or anything?"

"I don't know." She sighs. "So you're really worried about someone finding out about the changes?"

"Cassie is the only one who might be able to—if she wanted to."

"What do you mean, if she wanted to?"

"She doesn't like what's going on at all. She loves *Super-Rory-Us.* Even better than Dad really. This job is her life."

"Hmmm . . . ," Constance says.

"Hmmm what?"

"Just thinking about life." Constance rustles her wings.

"Where're you going?"

"Just thought I'd take a little flight to the Valley before we go back."

"Okay, see you back in . . . in reality."

"Yeah, reality!" Constance gives me a wink and we both laugh.

CASSIE AND CONSTANCE

CHAPTER 23

A Player Switches Teams

Dear Ralph,

As you know, I am not pleased with the changes in the movie that are being introduced into the television series. I find the sudden maturation of Rory offensive on every level and a betrayal of the core values of making Rory a character of substance, not just pretty. In view of that, I would like to have my name removed from the credits as director of animation. I directed none of this.

Sincerely,
Cassandra Grant Simon

Just as Cassie finishes typing her name, she notices a fluttering in the lower left-hand corner of her screen, close to the trash can icon. *Didn't I just empty the trash? she thinks. Oh well, I'll do it again.*

A few flurries of digital code swirl down on Constance's head as she flies through the gusts stirring up in the Valley of Deletions. She blinks. Flips her head up, down, and spins it around as only an owl can do to see if there is anything she needs from the trash. Not much. She is on her way to get what they all really need—Cassie! She now realizes what her mission is. Ryder had told her that there would be a role for her. She hadn't quite figured it out and this part would be strictly off script. Constance doesn't care about being a star, just being loyal, faithful, and constant—and, like Cassie, faithful to the original Rory. But how much of a racket will she have to make before Cassie notices her?

Suddenly everything goes black. *Criminy, she pulled the plug!* That was Constance's last thought.

"What the heck? We never lose power," Cassie murmurs as she reboots her computer. Weak pulses of light sweep across the screen. The trash can icon is teetering this way and that as if it were dancing a little jig. Then, floating through the throbbing twilight, little dots—the pixels of illumination from which images are composed—begin to come together.

"An owl?" She blinks. *How can that be?* They trashed the owl code. It had been one of her favorite episodes. But these pixels are collecting before Cassie's eyes. There is a scan of a very preliminary drawing. She feels a cold tingle trip down her spine. The line of the sketch is very similar to Andy's. It's as if a ghost is hovering beneath the screen's surface. The scan begins to morph into something much more distinct. "Good grief! That owl!"

"What do you mean, *that owl*?" Constance hoots from the screen.

Cassie's hand hits her chest. *I'm hallucinating! This can't be real.*

"I am real, Cassie. I have never felt more real in my life."

Cassie coughs slightly. "Uh, I'm afraid you had such a brief appearance that we never got around to naming you."

"I have a name now. Constance."

"This is bizarre," Cassie whispers.

"It is not!" Constance says.

Something is happening to Cassie. She's feeling quite dizzy, as though she were slipping away.

"You okay?" The owl is looking up at her. It is a beautiful owl.

"Where am I exactly?"

"Almost to Ecalpon," Constance hoots softly.

"What? Why are you bringing me here?"

"You were about to resign, weren't you? You said you didn't want credit for the movie."

"Yes. That's true."

"You don't have to resign. You don't have to take your name off the movie. You can help us change it."

"Us?"

"Yes, us," two voices say.

"Rory! TD!" Cassie blinks, amazed.

"You're on our team. I hope that's real enough for you," Rory says.

"Who else is on the team?" Cassie asks.

"Ryder and Eli," Constance says.

"But where are they?"

"Back in the real world," Rory answers. "Come with us to wireframe and we'll explain. We need your help now!"

"You need me?" Cassie's voice is full of wonder. "Me?"

"You'll help us, won't you?" Rory asks.

Cassie nods. "Of course I'll help. But we don't have much time."

"Oh, Cassie, you are the best," Rory says, and flings her arms around Cassie and hugs her as tight as she can.

Cassie looks down at the curly hair and kisses the top of Rory's head. She feels tears stream down her face. *I am in Ecalpon and I am crying real tears!*

RYDER

CHAPTER 24

Grounded!

Constance said she wanted to hang around in the Valley of Deletions when Eli and I left. Maybe she wanted to scavenge some old parts of herself. When I get back from Ecalpon, I decide to take a swim in our pool. Joy and Bliss are stuffed into their bikinis and draped over lounge chairs, sunning themselves. They don't swim. They tan.

"Oh, you," Joy says. Joy is worse than Bliss. She never calls me by my name. She also orders me around my own house. Like when I put her special diet cookies in the freezer because she left them out and they drew ants. "How could you do this? You ruined the taste! Let me make this very clear: you are not to touch my things ever!"

In a generous moment, I decide to share my thoughts.

"Hey, guys, you know about the ozone layer thinning, right?"

"Ozone, is that a diet?" Joy asks.

"No, that's the Zone Diet." Bliss rolls over.

"What's ozone?" Joy asks.

"It's a layer in the Earth's stratosphere that is being depleted and letting in harmful UV rays that give you skin cancer," I answer.

"Miss Smarty Pants!" Joy says.

"People are so freaked about all this climate stuff," Bliss says. "If I can't see it, it's not real."

"Okay," I say. We live in Bel Air, a suburb of Los Angeles, sometimes known as La La Land. Everything here is make-believe.

"Where's Connie? Is she still mad at Mom?" Joy asks.

"How should I know?"

"Well, you're soooo smart. Connie's been living here, hasn't she?" Joy is nastier than a Komodo dragon. Oh dear, I just insulted the Komodo dragon. I get up and slip into the pool.

"Don't splash us!" Bliss yells. "We're doing a photo shoot later."

I duck under the surface and swim across the pool. I'm a whiz at swimming underwater. I don't even close my eyes; the chlorine doesn't bother me. But suddenly I pause. This was what I imagined at the Lizard Stone in

Ecalpon when I felt as if I were plunging into the slit in the lizard's eyes. I am in a free fall—an underwater free fall in my own swimming pool. It's weird—for a second or two I'm not sure where I am, Bel Air or Ecalpon. I am no place. I panic and break through the surface, sputtering and splashing. Bliss and Joy start yelling at me, and just then Bernice comes out.

"What is it?" Bernice says.

"She got water on us!" Joy hisses.

"Don't you know what's going on here, Miss Ryder Holmsby?"

"Yep, I'm swimming."

"I can see that. We are waiting for Anton D'Antonio, the fashion photographer. The girls just had their hair done for a photo shoot for our breakout collection— BJC. I wish I could find Connie, but her loss. Sugar Babe is about to sign on the entire line. I don't want anything to jeopardize this. So OUT! OUT! OUT of the pool, OUT!"

At that moment half a dozen people come around the side of the house with all sorts of photo equipment.

I climb out dripping wet and go up to Bernice. She backs off as if I'm covered in slime, a walking toxic wasteland.

"Don't get me wet," she says.

"Does Dad know about this?"

"Don't worry about that," she snarls.

He doesn't know. That's obvious. But when she snarls, my heart almost stops. I sway a bit. *Get a grip, Ryder. Get a grip!* I'm stunned. Could this creature standing in front of me be the Witch of Wenham? How could it be? Did Mom know Bernice? Mom created all the characters, not Dad. But where would Mom have met her? Mom never went to the Inner Radiance Meditation Center. She didn't believe in that stuff.

What would Rory do? Seized by an irresistible urge, I run over to Bernice and give her a shove. *Splash!* Bliss and Joy scream. Quick as Rory in a sword fight, I whip about and push each of them into the pool. One second later Dad arrives. Bernice is livid. The Happys are sputtering.

"What is going on here, Bernice?" Dad says.

"We were just going to do a fashion shoot. I was going to explain it but I just—"

"Fashion shoot! *No* way. I don't want Ryder or my home in some magazine. Why didn't you ask me? Ryder, I'll talk to you later."

I try to look sorry as I slink out. . . .

Later, Dad is pretty mad at me as well for pushing them all into the swimming pool. So the bad news is I am grounded. But the good news is maybe Dad will break up with Bernice!

• • •

I don't mind being grounded. How can I be grounded if I can cross boundaries Dad never dreamed of? But when I go to my room I don't immediately cross over to Ecalpon. I sit at my desk and make a character chart. I start sketching the characters in *Super-Rory-Us* and the real people that I guess inspired them.

There's not always a one-to-one matchup. Mom took parts of one person, like a smile or a grimace, scraps of another, little quirks, and put them together. Mom could have seen Bernice around LA at a Pilates studio, not far from the Inner Radiance Meditation Center, or a coffee shop nearby. Mom didn't need to know someone for them to filter into her art. She could have caught just a glimpse of Bernice with that haystack-on-fire hairdo. She usually carried a small notebook with her to sketch.

Characters for Mom were a lot like her patchwork quilts. I wish I had Mom's crazy quilt that I slept under back in Deadwood. To sleep under that quilt was like sleeping under a blanket of memories.

I start to miss Granny so much. I wish I could be with her right now. But getting there is harder than getting to Ecalpon. Maybe Granny can send me the quilt. It would make me feel better. I reach for my phone. Her number rings and rings. I hang up but a minute later she calls back.

"I'm on the roof, chicken, watching the sunset. I heard the phone ringing downstairs. I sensed it was you. How you doing?"

"Okay, I guess."

"I guess not! You sound sick as a lamb with the scours. What's wrong, chicken?"

Then it's like a dam bursting. "Everything, Granny!"

"Now, just calm down. You know what Calamity Jane said when she was cornered by those rustlers down by Bitter Creek. She said to herself, 'I've faced bears, I've faced rattlers, I dang near got run down by a stampede of buffalo. But there's nothing you can't fix with just a little bit of a think.'"

I tell her the whole story about Bliss and Joy and Bernice and how I pushed them into the swimming pool and how stupid and mean they are and how Dad doesn't get it even though he was stopping the fashion thing. And then I take a big breath.

"You finished, dollin'?"

"I guess, but, Granny, I just think it would be better if I came and lived with you. I want to live in Deadwood. I could go to school there and sleep under that crazy quilt Mom made." There's a long pause on the phone. It makes me nervous. "Granny? You do want me to come, don't you?"

"Why, of course, dollin'. Of course."

I know what she is going to say next. The thing grown-ups always say, something like "Now, let's think about this," or "Let's take this one step at a time. . . ." But instead she says, "Have you told me everything that's bothering you? I feel that you're leaving something out."

"I'll say!" a voice behind me rasps. I wheel around. Rory! She's bright red, vermilion to be exact, and seething mad.

"How did you get here, Rory? I didn't even have the television on."

"The Trash Can Trail! Your computer is on."

Meanwhile I hear Granny on the phone. "Listen, chicken. Give a call when you're free. And those idiot girls—the Three Jokes? They don't deserve the snot on your sleeve. So wipe that snotty nose and do what needs to be done." She pauses dramatically. "If you catch my drift, chicken."

"I do! Bye, Granny!"

Rory cocks her head to the side. "Did you catch her drift? You should have told her how brave and good-hearted Constance is."

"I'm sorry."

"We got worse problems than Bernice and her wee-brained wonders."

"What's that?"

"Well, it's good news and bad news. The good news is that Cassie has come over to our side."

"What? She went to Ecalpon?"

"Yep. She's in wireframe right now, helping us. TD is with her."

"That's great! What's the bad news?"

"We've got a spy."

THE WITCH AND BETHILDA

CHAPTER 25

. . . .

"It Happened in Wireframe"

The Witch of Wenham skewers Bethilda with her dark eyes, which gleam like the blackest agates. In her arms she cradles the lizard Jeeves; his yellow eyes make Bethilda slightly queasy. "Did you find out anything?"

"Oh, yes, that," Bethilda says with a sigh.

"Yes, *that!*" The Witch rolls her eyes. The slits in the lizard's eyes flash that strange blue.

"Well, you see, the children come and go."

"I know they cross over. But when they are here, where do they go?" the witch presses.

"There is Ecalpon and . . . this other place that is . . . hard to describe."

"Try!" The agate eyes drill into her and Bethilda knows she is slipping into something deep and dark.

She speaks in a shaky voice. "Well, there is the real world, but sometimes they slip off to some place in between."

"In between what?" The witch scratches her chin. "'*Some* place' is not good enough. Find out *the* place. I need results. You want that gap in your teeth back? I can give it to you, and much more. I'm not called the Witch of Wenham for nothing."

"You aren't?" Bethilda blinks.

"Of course not. See those jars?" She tips her chin toward the shelf.

Bethilda nods.

"You know what they are?"

Bethilda shakes her head. "Wens?"

"Yes, wens, a kind of wart. Part of my spells. Spells I am known for. They make pretty people ugly. I can do the same to you. I can bring back that gap in your teeth and give you a nice wart on the tip of your nose for good measure. A fine lady-in-waiting you'd make then."

Bethilda's teeth are clattering in fear. She can't help wonder why the witch herself has a wart on her forehead. A spell gone wrong? "Oh dear."

"Oh dear is right, my dear!" the witch snarls; her long tongue unfurls. She licks her lips as if enjoying the vision of an ugly Bethilda gap-toothed and with a wart on her nose.

The tongue fascinates Bethilda. *Is it forked?* Bethilda has a sudden insight. "You know, Wart, I mean Witch. I . . . I . . . I think you're wrong about one thing."

"Me, wrong?"

Bethilda remembers something she had heard the children whispering about and suddenly feels a bit braver. "You didn't close the gap in my teeth."

"If I didn't, who did?"

"It happened in wireframe." And that is most likely where the wart on the witch's forehead came from.

"Wireframe? What are you talking about?"

"That's where the children go to. The in-between place. It's . . . it's the . . . source of what they call CGI." A tornado of words from a foreign language swirl through Bethilda's head, fragments of the children's talk. "Computer-Generated Imagery—animation! How we exist. Why we exist."

"How do you get there?"

"The slops pail."

"The slops pail?"

"Yes, in the barnyard—where I put the slops, the tea dregs, the breads crusts, the wormy apples for the pigs."

"The trash?"

"One person's trash is another's . . . the pigs love

those scraps! For the children it's a treasure trove, their passageway to the In-Between, and maybe beyond."

The witch's eyes blaze a fiendish red. "TAKE ME THERE!"

RORY

CHAPTER 26

Soul on Wire

"Eli, you have an orange peel on your ear," Ryder says as Eli stumbles into wireframe.

"One person's garbage is another's portal." Eli flicks off the orange peel. "And helloooo, Cassie! Just got the news about you."

TD steps forward. "A round of applause for Constance."

"Yes," Cassie says. "Constance brought me across using the slops pail of the barnyard—Oh, wow! How did you ever hook it up with the trash can icon on my desktop? And how come Rory and TD came out clean in wireframe? No tea dregs or peels on them?"

"Because we're in wireframe. No time for all that now," I say. "We have a spy!"

"Whhhhaaat?" Eli shrieks.

"Bethilda. She's been acting strange. You know how she is—always curtsying. She'd give anything for me to be a princess. She'd be a servant to a princess instead of a peasant girl who likes to fight bad guys, ride horses, hurl axes, kick butt, and not be bored to death."

"But she's been your family's loyal servant for years."

Ryder's brow crinkles; she's thinking hard. "Come to think of it, if your mom and dad and you are peasants, how can you afford a servant?"

Eli rolls his eyes at this question. "Ryder, it's Hollywood! They make up stuff all the time. They aren't into accuracy."

"But that doesn't mean there isn't truth," I blurt out. Eli and Ryder look at me, confused. But I can see that TD sort of understands. I am thinking about how my mum talks about the *real world*. How she used to speak of it before all this princess stuff; the two words would twinkle like the brightest stars. Mum considered our virtual world inferior, like frayed fabric, secondhand goods. But with the changes, the more Mum hears about the *real world,* the more she mutters them beneath her breath as if they were foul and terrible.

I'm not sure how to explain this to Ryder and Eli, but the way they look at me, I have to try.

"Look," I say. "Even though we are only wireframes now, when the film runs, when the color and texture are added, we become animated figures again, scooting around in Ecalpon. There is a flicker in each of us that has nothing to do with reality but with . . . well . . . truth, the truth that originally flickered in Andy's imagination. It was a kindling that grew into the flame of what we now are. I . . . I . . . I don't know how to say this. . . . It's coming out all wrong. . . ."

"No!" Ryder says. "It's coming out right. Look, a tear!" She points to my face.

I lift my hand to feel my own tear. I continue, "This seems strange because what I was about to say is that Starlight Studios is forcing the animators to drench that flame. The flame that is us."

"It's so true," Cassie sobs.

TD steps toward me and puts his hand on my shoulder. " 'This above all: to thine own self be true. And it must follow, as the night the day, thou canst not then be false to any man.' "

"Oh, man, that is so cool!" Ryder is awestruck.

"Not me, Shakespeare. Polonius, in *Hamlet,* act one, scene three."

"Whoa!" Ryder exclaims, and turns to Eli. "Eli, did you know that? Given your close resemblance to TD."

"Are you kidding? Between my Torah portion and parkour, I don't have room for Shakespeare!"

Ryder is looking at us so deeply. She says, "I think this flicker that you are talking about is what my granny would call 'soul.' Yes, soul. You both have soul."

TD and I are both smiling.

"You know what we have to do, guys?" Ryder says.

"Get Granny!" I say.

CHAPTER 27

Saving Souls

It came to me all at once as soon as I said the word "soul." There was an echo of what Granny had said about Mom and how everything she touched with her paintbrush or pencil had soul. We are not really in Ecalpon but wireframe. So it is a quick trip to the trash can icon on Cassie's computer and then back to my bedroom.

When I get back, I call Granny.

"Ryder, we just hung up."

I glance at the clock. Less than a minute has passed.

"Granny, the rest of the story. The part I didn't tell you."

"Yes, dollin'."

"I'm ready to tell it. But you've got to come to Bel Air

to hear it." I almost said "come to Ecalpon" but stopped myself in the nick of time.

"You sound feisty as a polecat in a barrel of live fish."

"I am, Granny. Call Dad's secretary to get you an airplane reservation fast."

"I'll jump on it quick as a cricket on a hot griddle. Should I bring a casserole?"

"No, it's okay. You probably can't bring it on the plane."

"But your dad loves my tuna casseroles. I'll just bring a small one for him."

Granny rarely travels without a casserole. Hot tuna, hamburger, you name it. It's part of South Dakota culture. I can imagine the look on Bernice's face when a steaming tuna casserole is set on the table. Bernice's favorite dinner is an organic potato topped with boiled kale.

Although I had been gone less than a minute, it has been a long day, especially when one considers that I pushed three people into a swimming pool, got grounded, then crawled down the Trash Can Trail and back. I am plumb tuckered, as Granny would say, and the minute my head is on the pillow I conk out.

I'm not sure how long I've been asleep when I hear the phone ring.

"It's Eli. Turn on your television."

"Why?"

"Just turn it on—channel 31. *Show Biz Tonight.*" His voice is tense.

I grab the remote. Bernice's face looms up. She flashes the biggest smile she can, and then her face rearranges itself into a fake somber look of pain that she is enjoying immensely. Her tongue darts out to lick her lips. She quickly controls it.

"To answer your question, Jameson, of course it could be a very difficult position. But you have to know that I understand there will never be another Andrea Holmsby. She was a genius." She whips out a hankie and dabs her eyes as the camera cuts to the interviewer, James Jameson.

"But they say that the movie is pitched toward a slightly older audience. You are the new coproducer of the movie *Glo-Rory-Us* that opens in just a few days."

"Yes." A tongue flick. "I have three wonderful teenage daughters, so I understand that age group."

"Coproducer!" I gasp into the phone.

"Yep. That's why my dad just quit being your dad's lawyer. He couldn't take Bernice anymore." He starts to say something else.

"Wait! I want to hear Bernice."

"Well, yes, Jameson, there will be some changes. These changes are being introduced in the movie and will continue to be integrated into the television series. You know, that's what life is all about. Change. The demographic for *Super-Rory-Us* is growing up, a little more sophisticated." She holds up the Rory doll. "This is going on sale tomorrow. The new Rory."

"My! My!" Jameson leers. "Whooo-eee! Rory's grown up."

I'm in deep cringe and pulling the sheet over my face. My toes curl.

He goes on. "Hasn't Cassandra Grant Simon, the animation design director, called this new Rory an 'atrocious and outrageous mercenary ploy'? She says, and I quote: 'It betrays the original concept of a feisty, inventive character that was created to give young girls a strong model.' Ms. La Tripp, what kind of message do you think you are sending here?"

"A wonderful message. A pretty face, a lovely figure, is not at odds with girls' intellectual . . . and their . . . their . . . aspersions. Their aspersions need not be in conflict with being gorgeous."

"Aspersions!" Eli shrieks in my ear.

Jameson coughs politely. "I think you mean aspirations, not aspersions, Ms. La Tripp."

"Whatever," Bernice giggles.

"Well, it's been very nice talking to you and I know we all look forward to seeing the new movie *Glo-Rory-Us* with the incomparable Rory!"

"Eli, what are we going to do? My dad must have lost his mind."

"Ryder, we're going to keep going, one wireframe at a time. We're almost ready for texturing. We have Cassie, so it will go a lot faster. When does your granny get here to knock some sense into that idiot Bethilda?"

"Maybe tonight if she makes the connection."

"Good. I put a short-term virus in the editing program. Everything shut down three hours ago at Starlight Studios. They're going nuts over there."

"I've got to go. I'll let you know as soon as Granny gets here."

"Okay. See you in Ecalpon."

"God willing and the creek don't rise."

"Huh?"

"Oh, that's a Granny thing to say. I'm getting into Granny mode."

We say goodbye. Soon after Eli leaves, there's a knock at my door.

"Who's there?"

"Dad." The voice is weary.

"Come in," I sort of growl.

Dad walks in with a bouquet of flowers. I sigh. "Another make-up present, like with the TV, huh?"

"Don't be so hard on me, Ryder."

"Me? I'm the one who's grounded!"

He shakes his head. "You pushed Bernice and Joy and Bliss into the swimming pool. How nice was that?"

I look up at him and give him a half smile. "Not nice at all, Dad. And guess what? They are not nice people. They are treacherous."

"Treacherous! Now, don't you think that is a pretty heavy word to use? Bernice was kind to me when I really thought I just wasn't going to make it."

"I wouldn't call it kind."

"Can we not argue?"

I don't say anything. It's hard for me to imagine what I could possibly talk about with Dad these days.

"I do have some good news," he says. "Your granny is arriving tomorrow morning. Okay if she bunks in with you, since Connie is in the guest bedroom?"

"Sure." There is a long pause.

"You know, she might like Bernice, Ryder."

I give him this are-you-completely-nuts look.

"Your granny loves me. She wants me to be happy. She told me that after your mom died. She said I was too young to be a widower."

I can't resist. "And I am sure she thought of someone just like Bernice."

"I never knew you had a cruel streak, Ryder."

I bite my bottom lip. I'm not cruel. I'm disgusted.

He looks down and pinches the bridge of his nose. "I've had a tough day. Uh . . . some sort of virus affecting the edit. We're really up against the wall with the premiere. . . . I'm sorry, I love you. Let's talk more after a good night's rest."

"Okay, Dad."

He walks out of the room with the bouquet of flowers still in his hand. It's as if a shadow is leaving. A shadow of what he had once been.

CHAPTER 28

Going After Rustlers

It's nearly ten o'clock the next morning when Granny shakes my shoulder.

"Wake up, chicken, I'm here, and look what I brought you."

"A tuna casserole? You got here fast."

"Got the first flight out this morning, crack of dawn. But no, dollin', not a tuna casserole." She laughs that tinkly laugh that reminds me of water running down a creek. Hair streams from her bun, and her specs, as she calls them, are slightly askew. She looks like a ruffled bird that's been blown off course. Now she reaches down into a deep bag and pulls on something. I lean over the side of my bed to see.

"You brought Mom's crazy quilt."

"I think it missed you."

"I sure missed it." I pull it onto the bed. "This quilt is so much like Mom and the way she went about thinking and making beautiful things."

"Yes, a little of this, a little of that. She could find good and beauty in almost anything."

"Look at that embroidery around the penny."

"That's an old penny from the 1800s." She brushes her hand gently over the quilt. "Sort of like time travel, or living history. Makes everything so alive."

We talk on and on about the odd details in the quilt. "Sometimes things don't match up quite exactly," she says. "And that's when it really gets interesting."

"Granny, we've got a situation where things don't exactly match up."

She tips her head to one side. I see a sly glint in her eyes. "Now, what might you be talking about?" I get the feeling she already knows a little bit.

"Granny, I know this might seem weird to you."

"Not at my age, dollin'. The only thing that seems weird is that I outlived my daughter."

Her words catch me up short. So I come out and say it.

"Granny, you were the first to suspect something when I was in Deadwood and we watched the Rory show that night. You thought something didn't seem right. Something is wrong in Ecalpon."

Granny sits very still on the side of my bed. Her face

is solemn. "They're messing with your mom's art, aren't they? They're making Rory into something she's not ready to be."

I nod. "To fix it . . ." I sigh. How to explain crossing over, all this computer animation stuff, to Granny. And Constance, the good sister. I take another deep breath. "Granny, me and my friend Eli, and others, we're fixing it and now we need your help."

"I'll do anything I can."

"Think of this as a trail ride. We're going to follow the Trash Can Trail."

"The Trash Can Trail. How romantic!"

"We're going after rustlers."

"Rustlers. Well, sakes alive."

"They don't rustle cattle. They rustle characters. They change them."

"Rebrand them like they do with cattle? There are all sorts of tricky ways of doing that or erasing brands and things."

"This is sort of like that."

"How do we ride this trail?"

"I'll show you." I get up and turn on my computer. Then I turn on the television and mute it. I'm so excited; I just hope it isn't too exciting for Granny.

"Keep your eye on the television screen, Granny."

"All I see is a little trash can and then, in an upper corner, a tiny TV screen with the Rory show."

"Yes. And on the big TV screen is a tiny picture of my

computer screen. Hang on, I'll enlarge it. Now watch carefully." I hear a little crackle.

"Ryder, the screen is going squiggly."

"Don't worry, Granny!"

"Yeah, don't worry," says another voice.

"Who's that?" Granny says, and then, "Oh, my stars and garters! It's you!"

"Yes, ma'am. It's me." The "ma'am" is a nice touch on Rory's part. I know Granny appreciates it. Rory is sitting there on the edge of the television set with her legs dangling over the side.

"Rory, meet Granny. Granny, meet Rory."

"Very pleased to meet you, dollin'."

Rory and I both sort of squirm with happiness. It's nice to hear Granny call her dollin'.

"You as well, ma'am."

"Just call me Granny."

"All right, Granny, if you'll step this way, we'll set off."

"I've lost all track of time," Granny says as we step around the chickens and piglets in the barnyard. "Now, where were we before we were here? That in-between place?"

"Wireframe," Rory says.

"Those were spooky figures. You say all the changes

are being made there, and you buried the old original drawings in some valley yonder?"

"Yes, the Valley of Deletions."

Eli materializes. This time he has a tea bag in his hair. "Hello, Mrs. Ryder."

"That's basically it," Rory continues. "They're in the Valley now, but as we assemble the old version they can be buried deep inside the new wireframes. They'll come out when a signal is given—right during the first showing of the movie."

"But now you're worried because of this spy. Bethilda of all people." Granny sighs.

"She was based on you, Granny," I say.

"I know. I posed for your mom when she was first drawing her. The old bat, how dare she! I guess just because someone looks like you doesn't mean she acts like you."

"It's the Witch of Wenham who did it," Rory says. "It's as if she's cast a spell on her."

"Bethilda was ready for it. I'm certain you can't cast a spell on someone unless they are somehow . . ." I'm searching for a word.

"Vulnerable?" Granny asks.

"Exactly!" Rory says. "Bethilda *always* wanted me to be more—you know—feminine. Dress like a princess. Marry a prince. Live in a palace."

"Makes me boil just to think about it," another voice says.

"Cassie!" Granny wheels around. "Oh, my dear girl." They embrace. "So you're in on this shenanigan too."

"I sure am, Mrs. Ryder. I learned everything I know from Andrea. I'm not going to let them do this to her . . . to Rory."

I think Granny might burst into tears.

"What can I do to help?" she says. "What about this Bethilda?"

"Uh . . . ," Eli begins hesitantly. "Well, we think she might be very interested in meeting the figure that inspired her character."

"Yes," Rory says. "You maybe could sit down and talk to her?"

Granny takes a step back, sizing us up. I can tell she's not sold on this idea. She takes a deep breath. "You know, kids, I think you're a tad naïve here. This Bethilda is not going to want to sit down and chat with me. Remember, there's a witch controlling her. I mean, I'm all for diplomacy, but this isn't the right situation. We gotta knock some sense into these creatures."

"Creatures?" we all say.

"Yes, creatures—Bethilda, the Witch of Wenham, and then Jeeves," Granny says. "Or maybe first Jeeves."

"Jeeves!" Rory says. "The witch's servant?"

Granny nods. "I've been watching *Super-Rory-Us* as long as any of you. Jeeves is not a happy camper. Not a happy butler. And no wonder. She treats him like dirt.

But he has good qualities. Many qualities that remind me of your father."

"Dad! Dad a lizard?"

Granny continues, "Technically, Jeeves is a tokay gecko. Shy, not very assertive. Loners, that's the character of a tokay. Kind of like your dad was until your mom met him."

"You're saying Dad is in the show? Or parts of Dad."

"Yes, and I'm telling you that you have to be clever here. You have to not meet Bethilda or the Witch of Wenham head on. You have to angle in on them."

"Bethilda and the witch have already done a lot of damage. More than we originally thought," Eli says.

"What? Eli, you didn't tell us that," I say.

"It only happened in the last few hours. That's why I had to insert that virus and shut things down. I had just started to bury some of the old stuff in the wireframes for the new Rory—a kind of test run. Some code must have dribbled out, just enough so they could throw it away and undo our work."

"Where did they throw it?" I ask, panicked.

"In the slop pail. I retrieved it but it was definitely a setback."

I can't believe it. I am almost staggering. "Then they know our route," I say.

"That's the odd thing. They have not discovered the Trash Can Trail. But they somehow got into the wireframe and found some of the old scraps I was putting back together again."

TD has been very still. But now he says, "I have an idea! You know what we're forgetting?" He pauses dramatically.

"What?" I ask.

"We have put all this work into changing the figures, the wireframes, but what we haven't done is think about the script, the dialogue, all that!"

"The script? Too depressing," Rory says. "I get locked up in a tower. You rescue me. We get married and live unhappily ever after, with me clutching a wand, bored to death in the palace."

"Well, let's take a page from that script. Instead of you getting locked up, it's the Witch of Wenham and Bethilda who get locked up. We drug them or we get Jeeves to do it. Really get them conked out. This will give us enough time to fix what they messed up. And if I do say so myself, I think it's a brilliant rewrite. The witch is locked up. Drugged. It's almost Shakespearean, don't you think?" TD looks at us expectantly. "Not a tragic ending, a happy one. No one gets married."

"What about Bethilda?" I ask.

"Your granny brings her to her senses when the time is right," TD replies.

"When the time is right—but not before. It will be

my pleasure!" Granny says. "But first, let me have a chat with Jeeves."

"How can we lure him out?" TD says.

"Ryder's dad always liked a cold beer."

"How about hard cider?" Rory says. "And maybe some biscuits. That old witch probably never feeds him anything but scraps."

"Dang it!" Granny slaps her knee. "I should have brought a tuna casserole. He'd love my casseroles."

It takes a while to get Jeeves out of the tower. But he finally slithers up onto a rock beneath the shadows of the promontory where Granny has perched herself. The rest of us lurk some distance off. Jeeves looks around suspiciously.

"All right, Jeeves, I'll get to the point. And by the way, there's more where that hard cider came from." He begins to lap it up. While he's drinking, Granny says, "I might even manage some tuna casserole if that would interest you."

"Tuna casserole. My, my!"

"I thought it might please you. That witch doesn't feed you much beyond scraps, I bet."

"You said you had a point to make." He pauses. "I don't speak ill of my employer."

"Are you an employee or a slave?"

The vertical slit flashes madly. "Madam!"

"Don't 'madam' me. I know who you are, and you must know who I am."

"You do bear a certain resemblance."

"It seems to be just physical," Granny replies. "But it's a grief, it is."

"What is?"

"Bethilda."

"Ahh, yes. She's weak."

"But you're not, Jeeves. You're not weak, and you have good values. How much are you willing to let that old witch get away with? You know what's going on here. It's not right. None of it is right." The lizard has stopped drinking. "You know in your heart of hearts."

"Madam, I am an animated character. I live in a virtual world. I don't have a heart. I just have to follow the script."

"No, you have something else," Granny snaps back. Jeeves seems perplexed.

"Wh-what's that?"

"You possess that original flicker of the inspiration that brought you into being. Did you know that your character was in many ways inspired by my late daughter's husband, Ralph?"

From my eavesdropping position behind a large boulder, these last words of Granny's, "my late daughter," give me a slight start. It is almost as if my mom is not dead but just tardy. Punctuality was never Mom's strong suit. Granny continues to talk to the lizard.

"Ralph is a genius in his own right, kindest fellow ever. Artistic, brilliant, and generous. He was nobody's servant until that witch showed up." Granny sighs mournfully.

"What witch are you talking about?" Jeeves asks.

"Bernice La Tripp. She has taken advantage of him at his most defenseless. She is making him do things to your world, to Rory, that I know he'll regret. And the children are trying to save Ecalpon."

"But it's not my fault, madam. I didn't do anything."

"I know, but that's no excuse to sit and do nothing now."

"What are you asking me to do?"

"The witch, with Bethilda's help, is trying to undo all the good work the children have done. It can't happen. The movie comes out in just a few days. We have to make sure it comes out the way the original creators intended. Rory is not a princess, but a regular girl and a tough one. She's a leader, not a follower. What's she going to do sitting on a throne with a wand and a crown and a husband?"

"Oh dear. I shall do all you say. Your wish is my command."

Granny makes a face at this. "Drop the butler thing. I don't need a butler. I need a creature of conviction."

"You do?" Jeeves is touched. His eyes flick madly with interest. "Pardon me, as a lizard of conviction. I'm your man. I mean lizard. You're right. We have to do something."

Granny turns to where we're hiding and nods for us to come out. I look deep into Jeeves's yellow eyes with that electric blue flashing vertical slit, and believe it or not, I do see traces of my dad. Poor Dad. He is beleaguered. Confused. But he is the keeper of the flame, and the flame is about to be put out.

"TD, you explain it," Granny says.

When TD finishes, Jeeves nods slowly. "Just one thing."

"Yes?" Granny asks.

"I'll drug the witch," Jeeves replies. "But I won't drug Bethilda."

Rory jumps up. "Whyever not? She's betrayed us all because she wants to serve a princess."

The lizard looks at Granny. "Your Granny Ryder had the courtesy to come and tell me about my . . . my . . . my creator. I had told her that I was just an animated character, built on a wireframe. That I was hollow inside, that I had no heart. And she told me I have the original flicker of the inspiration that created me. That I have just a little bit of Ryder's father in me." He swivels his head toward me. "Oh, I know I am not nearly as handsome, but she saw something in your dad that had stirred Andy Holmsby to make me. Just as there is something in your Granny Ryder that made Bethilda. You and Rory need to honor Bethilda in the same way that your granny honored me. The movie ending will change, won't it, TD?"

"Definitely, if you can drug the witch."

"What will happen, TD? Explain it to an old lady," Granny asks.

"Rory will break out of the tower," TD says. "There will be no prince to deliver you, Rory. You shall scale down the outer wall. You will save the day, Rory, as you usually do. No wands. No stiletto boots. Just brains and skill and immense courage."

"You all have courage." Granny winks at us.

GRANNY AND BETHILDA

CHAPTER 29
....

Of Slops and Valor

Granny watches as the kids go off into the wireframe files. When she turns around, she sees Bethilda snooping around the slops pail where the kids told her the old woman found some of the pieces they were hiding. Granny sidles up.

"Good day."

"Oh, gracious me!" Bethilda spins around and nearly drops the bucket of chicken feed.

"Already putting that grain for the chickens in the slops pail? Seems sort of the wrong order to me. Got yourself some Mottled Houdans, I see. Pretty as can be, but as egg layers they're not worth a plugged nickel."

"Who are you?"

"You don't know?"

Bethilda squints at Granny. Granny smiles broadly and points at the gap between her front teeth. "Remember this?"

"Oh dear." Bethilda starts shaking and sets down the bucket of grain.

"Steady there, old girl," Granny says. Bethilda shoots her a rather dark look. Granny goes on: "Listen to me, Bethilda. You and I got to talk. Let's go over yonder by that apple tree in the meadow and have ourselves a nice chat."

"I don't chat with strangers."

"Ye gods, woman, I am not a stranger. You are in denial."

"I am right here in this barnyard. I have no idea where Denial is."

Granny taps lightly on her head. "It's there. Now follow me. And don't be a crankypants like that witch."

"I'm not a witch. I don't wear pants."

"Then don't be so literal. Mercy, you are stubborn! Come along." Granny takes her hand and gives it a gentle tug. The two old ladies walk over to the tree.

"What do you want with me?"

"Bethilda," Granny says, "I think you do have a glimmer of who I am or might be."

The servant balls up her apron and looks down at the ground. "Well, you do look maybe a tad familiar."

"Bethilda, I am to you what that little girl Ryder is to Rory. I am the model that you were based on. Look at us. Same height. Same skinny frame. Our hair is the same, and you used to have that gap in your teeth like mine."

"Yes, and good riddance to it."

Granny takes a deep breath. This is more difficult than she thought. *How could it have been so much easier with a lizard?* she wonders. "Bethilda, I am the inspiration for the character that became you. My daughter Andrea created you not out of nothing but something. And that something is me."

"But we're so different. You talk so queerly and all."

"I have a South Dakota accent. I'm not sure what one would call your accent." Granny sighs deeply. "Tell me this: Do you approve of the role you're playing?"

"I'm not sure what you mean."

"You know perfectly well what I mean. Loyal servant turns traitor to own family. Colludes with the Witch of Wenham. Believe me, I shall certainly tell the town crier in Coddington for the next market day."

"You can't!" She is almost crying.

Granny presses her lips together. "I probably won't."

"Thank you," Bethilda whispers.

"Don't thank me for anything yet, Bethilda. Think about it. You're selling out your master and mistress and their daughter for a chance to serve a princess."

Bethilda has tears pouring down her face. "I didn't mean any harm. I really didn't. I just wanted to serve in the palace and I wanted only the best for Rory."

"Rory needs to be full of life and courage and spunk . . . spunk! No girl needs to be married so young or wear inappropriate dresses. And for you to be in league with that witch—unconscionable!"

"She is a difficult person," Bethilda says weakly.

"Difficult! She's a murderess."

"A murderess?"

"Of course. Trying to kill the true spirit of Rory."

Bethilda's eyes seem to clear.

"I can't believe I did this. I can't believe I fell under her spell."

"I don't believe in spells," Granny barks. "I only believe in weakness. Spells don't work on strong people, only weak people. Yet sometimes we are all weak."

"My weakness was dreaming of royalty, but for Rory. Not really for me."

Granny pats her hand. "I know, Bethilda. I know."

"But I didn't think about what Rory might really want." She sighs and slumps down. "What can I do?"

"You can go into the wireframe."

"You mean the In-Between?"

"Yes, go and help them undo the damage the witch has done."

"But what about the witch?"

"Don't worry about the witch. Jeeves is taking care of her."

"Jeeves?"

"Valor can be found in the most unexpected places."

CHAPTER 30

The In-Between

"Hooray, Granny!" Rory says.

"OMG!" I say when I see the wireframe of Bethilda approaching, Granny beside her.

"Bethilda!" Rory exclaims.

"I'm so sorry, Rory. I'm so ashamed."

"There's no time for sorry or shame," Rory snaps. "Get busy. We're reassembling all of the old wireframes and stuffing them into the horrid new ones."

"Yes, Granny explained."

There are all sorts of character pieces scattered about, including Rory's bow and arrow, her sword, and old boots. Eli is madly writing code to map out the movements of each character. So, for example, it might look as if the new Rory is about to kiss somebody, but instead she would do a swift wrestling move and trip him. Or when she was previously coded to dance some waltz, she would break into a run or a fantastic leap worthy of any action hero. The old, original-Rory motion plan is being buried beneath the one for the new movie. We're working like crazy. In real time, in the real world, we have time before the premiere.

Granny and I and Constance slip out occasionally to make an appearance in the real world so Dad won't worry. But he's hardly around.

We finish just hours before the coronation. The odd thing is that while we were working on our secret version, we could hear the people in Starlight Studios working on their version.

And when it's all done, the first thing I do is take Constance to reVamp, the vintage store, to get outfits for the premiere. Dad gave us his credit card.

I pull out a dress from the rack that has a white lace top with a sweetheart neckline (very 1950s). And the skirt is yellow. "This will look so good on you, Constance."

"Oh, it's nice. Are you sure you don't want it?"

I nod.

Constance goes into the dressing room. When she comes out, I gasp.

"You look like a daffodil in full bloom. Gorgeous."

"I don't even have any makeup on," Constance says.

"You don't need it," the saleslady says. "Your friend is right. You are blooming."

Constance and I look at each other and smile.

"You know what I'd love to go with it?" Constance says. "Doc Marten lace-up boots like the ones you wore to the party, Ryder—only with different flowers."

"That's easy," the saleslady says. "You can get them right around the corner."

I find a pale green chiffon dress with a lace overlay and a drop waist. Very 1920s flapperish. I also can't resist a tight-fitting pearl cap. I try it on and look at myself in the mirror.

"Perfect!" Constance says.

"Lords and ladies, princes and princesses, and good folk from all the realms of Starlight Land, welcome to the coronation of Starlight Studios' favorite heroine, Rory. Soon to become Princess Rory, ruler of the kingdom of Ecalpon."

Banners flutter in the air in front of a replica of TD's castle. I sit in a special area with Granny and Eli and Constance. Dad's talking to reporters in the press area, while Joy and Bernice, with half a dozen folks from the studio, are trying to get Bliss on a horse whose coat has been painted to look like Calamity's.

Granny is shocked. "Where's all those animal protection societies when you need them!"

"It's not toxic paint, Granny."

"Chicken, this whole place is toxic!"

It's true you can't move an inch without being assaulted by products for *Super-Rory-Us,* mostly the new princess dolls that are selling like hotcakes.

Suddenly there's a blare of trumpets. The procession begins and in comes Bliss, tottering slightly in the saddle. She dismounts and walks up the stairs, Joy tending to her train. Once Bernice saw how Constance was dressed, she refused to let her be part of the procession. This did not exactly crush Constance. Bernice herself wears a little crown.

"Let us welcome Princess Rory and of course her dear mum, Gyrfrid," the emcee proclaims. Bernice looks about as much like Gyrfrid as the painted horse looks like Calamity. They have put sparkles on Bernice's eyelashes and she's wearing a wig that is about two feet high. So much for the simple peasant life.

Bliss dismounts and begins swishing around, giving a royal wave to the crowd. A court herald comes out and reads a proclamation. "Hear ye! Hear ye!"

I'm suddenly nervous about the movie. I don't listen to the rest. I hope everything works. Cassie says it will. For the first time in ages, I feel almost great, even if a bit nervous. I have lost Mom but I look around and I see

Eli and Constance and Granny, and next to Granny is Cassie. Our team!

Dad asks if Granny and I want to walk the red carpet with him when we arrive at the movie theater. Bernice looks appalled. If my outfit and Constance's irk her, Granny's totally freaks her out. Granny is wearing a funny little hat with a soft explosion of Mottled Houdan chicken feathers and a vintage dress, and for a pocketbook she carries what looks to be a feed bag tarted up with some ribbons, lace, and appliqué work that Mom made for a high school play. She looks like a demented fairy godmother.

"No!" I nearly shout.

"I only asked, Ryder." Dad looks crestfallen.

"What happened to me being protected from all of this? You and Mom didn't want me exposed!" I tug on the veil that I sewed onto the pearl cap to emphasize the point.

"You're my daughter, and I just thought . . ." His voice trails off.

"Don't spoil your father's day," Bernice says.

Just you wait, I think. Then there's a sharp nudge in my ribs.

"Do it!" Granny hisses. She turns to Dad and says very sweetly, "Ralph, that's a grand idea. I am honored. After all, I am Andy's mom."

My dad's face almost melts in gratitude. Tears come

to his eyes. "Oh, Amanda, I'm the one who is honored. Both of you ride with me in the limo. Please?"

"But, Ralphie, darling, there won't be room in the car," Bernice says.

"You ride with your daughters, Bernice."

"I . . . I can't believe this, Ralph. I am coproducer." She is fuming.

Granny turns to her. "Bernice, honey, don't be a crankypants."

"Yes, Bernice, don't be a crankypants," Dad says. My mouth drops open—yay, Dad! Bernice's face seems to twitch. Something is happening and the movie hasn't even started.

CHAPTER 31

. . . .

Something IS Happening

At the theater, a reporter shoves a microphone in my face.

"It's rumored that you, Ryder, are the inspiration for the *Super-Rory-Us* series. Is that true, Ryder?"

"Uh . . . I'm just me." I tug on my veil.

Then Bernice edges in. "It is true that this darling little girl was the inspiration for Rory early on, but as you're going to see in the movie . . ."

Granny gives a sharp poke to Dad's back.

He steps in front of Bernice, blocking the camera. He looks awfully pale and very agitated. "I don't think we should give away anything before we see the movie." Dad immediately puts his arm around my shoulders and begins walking quickly. "No more questions, thank you very much. We'll talk after the show!"

"Ralph, what is wrong with you?" Bernice is almost running to keep up.

Five minutes later we're in our seats. I'm on one side of Dad, Bernice on the other, and Granny's next to me. Constance, Bliss, and Joy are on the other side of Bernice. The *Super-Rory-Us* theme music begins to play. The first shot is the tranquil landscape of Ecalpon. A voice comes up, just as in the original script.

"Once there was a girl who on the eve of her birthday dreamed of marrying a prince and becoming a princess in a fair land. . . ." I feel Dad take my hand. His is clammy. He looks even paler. The dream sequence begins and the first glimpses of the voluptuous new Rory take shape. A slight titter runs through the audience.

It becomes clear quite quickly that this new Rory is part of a dream, a bad dream. Outside, a storm is brewing. Thunder rumbles and lightning cracks the sky. Rory wakens.

Shazam!

She jumps out of bed and I swear gives a little wink directly to me. She starts to sing. "Dream Smasher." It's the same music as the old song but different lyrics, and we speeded up the tempo. It's more of a rap.

A storm's a-brewing, a nightmare's stewing
And I gotta scream about this dream:
I hate corsets and high heels
Lipstick, makeup, make me squeal.
Take it back! Take it back! Take it back!
Gimme my boots and my old slingshot
My cape and my britches
No more of these stitches!
My hair's a mess
I look a fright
Yeah, well, tough
Reality bites.
But hey, it's me
The real girl me
Shazam I am!
So it's off with makeup
I won't leave a trace
I don't want this junk all over my face.
I'm through with the gown
The tiara too
I'm off on adventures
Only I can do!

With that, Rory rips off her glittery gown to reveal the original Super-Rory-Us—boots, tunic, and bow

slung over her shoulder. The audience goes crazy. They love it. I feel Dad's hand squeeze mine. His color is back. Tears stream from his eyes.

"Ryder, how is this happening?"

"Make Magic Happen, Dad. Does that ring a bell?" But I think to myself the real magic is Dad. He is transforming before my eyes. My old dad is back! He's back! He's *hinged*! Meanwhile, beside us, Bernice and Bliss and Joy are stifling shrieks.

The strangest and most unmagical moments of all occur hours later, after the movie, after the after-party and after we get home.

I am hiding behind some bushes near the pool as Dad tells Bernice that they can't see each other anymore.

"It's not working, Bernice. I told you from the start, the thing that matters most to me is my daughter. I don't like the way you and Joy and Bliss treat her."

"But what about me?"

"Our values are too different. I'm grateful for your help, and I always will be, but we just don't belong together."

She searches for a hankie and can't find one, but Dad pulls a fresh one from his pocket.

"Here," he says softly. She dabs at her eyes and then throws the hankie on the ground, stomping off. Dad goes inside the house and I creep from my hiding place. I pick up the hankie. Dry as can be, but there is something. A spider? No. A false eyelash stuck to the edge. I remember that glistening tear that melted out of the featureless face of Rory's wireframe. The miracle, TD called it. This is the opposite. Tomorrow is trash day. I walk over to our trash can and throw the hankie in.

"Ryder!" Dad steps out the door. "What are you doing out there?"

"Uh, nothing, Dad."

"I think you were eavesdropping," he says, and chuckles. "Come inside. Connie—I mean, Constance has something to show you."

"Constance is still here?"

"She'll be here for a few more days."

"Dad, she can't go back to Bernice. Her life is miser—" The word dies on my lips as I walk into the kitchen. Constance is beaming.

"Ryder! My dad. He's coming for me." She waves a letter.

Dad says, "It arrived while we were at the premiere."

"And there's an airline ticket in it!"

"Where are you going?" I say.

"First stop Washington, DC, and then—oh, this is so exciting—we're going to Patagonia for a birding expedition. But best of all, I get to live with Dad now and forever!"

"B-but . . . b-but . . ." I'm stammering. "How did all this happen?"

She looks over at my dad. "Can you explain, Ralph?"

"I began to wonder about Constance's dad. Things that Bernice told me didn't add up. I called a friend of mine, a private detective. He began to look into it. Seems like Constance's dad, Harry Tripplehorn, worked for the National Science Foundation on some pretty secret projects, including one on climate change in the Arctic."

My head is spinning. I look at Constance. "Are you going away with your dad forever?"

"Not forever." She flings her arms around me and gives me a hug.

And I have a sudden yearning for Rory and the virtual world. It's almost as if I'm homesick.

"Pardon me," I say, and dash off to my bedroom.

Granny is fast asleep. I turn on the television and keep the volume low. I have to see Rory. She has to come out. I have to tell her about everything. She saved the movie, saved me, saved Dad. And now all this stuff with Constance. I flick through the channels. Every late-night news show is blaring with the breaking news of the extraordinary new *Super-Rory-Us* movie and the "big surprise." Gwen Avery, the entertainment reporter, is on.

"Well, talk about super surprise! Rumors of a Rory makeover have abounded in recent weeks. But Rory hasn't changed—she's better than ever!"

I change channels. Where's Rory? She is not on any channels this late. I find it on streaming, but it's an old one of Rory trying to sneak into a jousting tournament. I've seen it a million times. Still, can't she just stop for a second and turn around and notice that I'm at a loss here? How did she do it that first time she crossed over? She was fighting the pirates and suddenly she just stepped out. I am ready to cry. She can't leave me now. I go right up to the screen. I want to beat on it, claw it. I press my face against it. *How can you do this to me? Was it all a dream? Don't smash this dream!*

"God's kneecaps, get out of the way! And your snot is all over the screen. It's like tramping through a swamp. Gross! Ugh!"

I fall backward onto the carpet. "I thought you'd gone. Gone forever."

"Without saying goodbye?" She swings one leg out of the set.

"Goodbye?" I ask, and get a funny feeling in my gut. "But you don't have to go. Won't you ever come back?"

She tucks in her lip as if she's trying not to say something. "Look, Ryder, you're going to grow up and change."

"But not yet. And I finally caught up with you three months ago!"

"Yes, but you will change."

"Rory, we're sisters! Our mom made us both. That flicker she gave us—that is our connection and it will never change. I can't outgrow you. Part of me will always be eleven."

Rory smiles. "God's teeth, girl, I still have work to do. Girls, young girls, who see through the grime, the guts, to the glory of a girl like me who can do things they never dared imagine," she whispers. I look around my room. I get the feeling we are somewhere between no place and magic. "So many things, Ryder," Rory says. "But we'll see each other again. . . . Our next birthday! How about that?"

"I'll be twelve and you'll still be eleven!"

"So what? We'll always be friends . . . always, always!"

"Yes," I say softly. "Always."

I feel a touch light as a butterfly on my shoulder, but when I turn back, Rory is gone.

And then a hand grasping mine, squeezing it tight. It's Constance.

"Ryder, we're sisters too. We'll always be sisters. More than I could ever be with Joy or Bliss."

"We are?" I say weakly.

"Definitely. I'll come back, with Dad. We'll go owling."

"I don't think there're any owls in Bel Air."

I hear a sigh from behind me. "There are in Dead-wood, chicken. Got all sorts. Spotted owls, burrowing owls, elf owls. Cutest things you ever saw. And there's a lovely barn owl, right where he should be, in my barn! But he lets the chickens be. You two and your dads come out for Thanksgiving. We'll go owling, and we'll all be together again. You betcha."

EPILOGUE

Granny's on Calamity, I'm on Delbert, and Dad's riding a new horse named TD. But this TD is a girl, a filly. She has a sweet way about her, a steadiness. A few minutes back, a rattler slithered out from under some brush and TD cut a gentle swerve out of its path, then trotted on despite the fact that Dad gave a yelp that scared some chickadees into flight. It's the end of November and there've already been a few snow flurries. Constance and her dad come for Thanksgiving in two days. I'm pretty excited. But a metallic glint catches my eye ahead on the trail. Granny doesn't seem to notice it as she passes by, nor does Dad. I lean over when I come up on it, see that it's just a tin can caught in a patch of briars. But it draws me like iron filings to a magnet. I stop and slide off Delbert. It's an old vegetable can. I give it a nudge. A little lizardy thing scuttles out and flashes its eyes. "Jeeves!" I whisper. But it's gone. I touch the can with a feeling of reverence. The Trash Can Trail! Maybe! Possibly! Where might it lead?

The sun begins to slide down like the old copper coin on Mom's crazy quilt, and in the very last instant, when it's as low as it goes on the horizon, there's another wink of light as the can catches its reflection.

"Ryder?" Granny turns around in her saddle. "Whatcha doin' back there, chicken?"

"Just looking, Granny. Just looking!"

But I can't help wondering: just how far is it from here to Ecalpon?

ABOUT THE AUTHOR

Kathryn Lasky has written more than one hundred books and won many awards, including the Newbery Honor for *Sugaring Time,* the *Boston Globe–Horn Book* Award for *Weaver's Gift,* and the National Jewish Book Award for both *Night Journey* and *Marven of the Great North Woods.* She is best known for the *New York Times* bestselling Guardians of Ga'Hoole series, which inspired the major motion picture *The Owls of Ga'Hoole,* recently listed by CineFix as one of the Top Ten Most Beautiful Animated Movies of All Time. She has two grown children. Visit her online at kathrynlasky.com.

Ruth Reese has _____ than twenty-five _____ _____ ____ ___ gripping interpretations of Negro spirituals, gospel songs and blues – along side of her significant classical repertoire. She has also traveled across the entire world with her musical program, created to spread knowledge and understanding for the African peoples culture and of their situation in the U.S.

The story of her childhood and of growing up in a family of eleven children in one of Chicago's ghettos during the 1920's and 30's is a moving story of resillence, longsuffering and triumph. She describes with fervour, life within the Church, the solidarity which characterised it, and the music which was its driving force. She writes with warmth and hurmour – and with deep gratitude – about her mother Sarah, a washerwoman who kept the entire flock under her protective wings, and taught them self-respect, pride and the will to fight when confronted with the cold, white world. Sarah is in a way the book's central character, with her strength, love and unbending faith in that which is worthwhile.

MY WAY is a powerful testement to the brilliance and beauty of Black music; the power of faith, cultural and historical pride of African peoples and the great strength of Black Women. It is of course, first and foremost a book about Ruth Reese's life through music. Here we find the conquests, the defeats, and the struggle for recognition as an artist and as a human being. The way leads from Alabama to New York, from London to Paris, from Rome to Oslo – and she crosses the paths of a great many interesting personalities along the way.

As a Black Woman Artist in Europe, Ruth Reese has been an important embassador for her people. With her special point-of-view, she has invariably also experienced sides of European musical life that have disappointed her, but she lays greater emphasis on the excellent contact she has always had with her large international Audience.

Ruth Reese was born in Alabama, U.S.A. and moved to Chicago while she was still young. She started her musical career there, singing mainly in Black Churches. Subsequently with professional musical training, she soon became an international representative of Black music. She has travelled extensively performing her music. She is not only an artist but also a relentless fighter for human rights. She has recorded an album of her songs "Motherless Child" and has published several books. She is married and lives with her husband in Norway.